Kay Darling

Kay Darling

Laura MacDonald
&
Alex Pugsley

Coach House Press
Toronto

Coach House Press
50 Prince Arthur Avenue, Suite 107
Toronto, Canada M5R 1B5

FIRST EDITION
Printed in Canada

"Kay Again" appeared in somewhat different form in *The Idler*.
"Will" appeared in somewhat different form in *Blood & Aphorisms*.

Published with the assistance of the Canada Council, the Ontario
Arts Council, the Department of Canadian Heritage and the Ontario
Publishing Centre.

Canadian Cataloguing In Publication Data
MacDonald, Laura, 1963–
        Kay darling
ISBN 0-88910-476-X
I. Pugsley, Alexander Hunter, 1963–
II. Title.
PS8575.D65K3 1994   C813'.54   C94-930318-6
PR9199.3.M33K3 1994

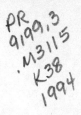

To Don Rossiter

Kay Darling

To: Kenneth Jansen, Liane Pecca
Fr: Kay Pritchard
Re: Resignation
Dt: Friday, February 2, 1991
Cc: Yvonne Lee, Davis Brewer

As many of you now know, this morning I met with Kenneth to give formal notice of my resignation. I wish to explain my reasons for leaving Gryphon Films.

I want you to know that my decision to resign is not related to yesterday's meeting nor is it a reflection of the objections I raised regarding the post-production on EMMA'S STORY. I have been developing an independent project for the last year and hope to use the next few months to complete it. Because editorial consensus was elsewhere, i.e. because Gryphon has decided not to develop the project, I have decided to try to get it off the ground another way. Put plainly, it's time for me to devote myself exclusively to finishing my own project.

My two and a half years at Gryphon have contributed immeasurably to my experience and I wish you all continued success.

Yours truly,
Kay Pritchard

4564 rue Clarke
Montreal, Quebec
H2T 2T4

February 28th. My second night

Dear Judith:
Spent the last hour trying to hook up my printer and finally realized it was LPT2 not LPT1 like it was supposed to be. I thought that little envir virus that took me hours and hours to disinfect from all my disks last year had come back to get me. This will have to be a quick note because it's really late and I have to get up early tomorrow to let in the Bell Canada guy to get my own phone hooked up and run a dozen errands.

Well, I've been très très busy packing and moving in. I am completely fed up with Toronto. I've had the most horrible winter of my entire life and I just need a break. I am burnt out. It was full of so many ridiculous complications with which I'd managed to fuck up my life: work, that loser, lecher, sleazo and jerk-off, Davis Brewer, Will, even Peggy Scofield, and Jordan, of course, and his pals. Individually his friends are quite lovely, but as a group they have run out of things to say to each other, so they make clever quips and joke around what they really want to say. You will be glad to know that before I left I told him I couldn't help him anymore with his new girlfriends and all his emotional baggage. It was bad enough that we spent two years in limbo, trying to decide whether he should move out or not. But to endure six more months of him talking about someone else is too much. I've decided that Jordan doesn't really want a girlfriend, he just wants a lot of worthless heart-to-hearts about whether he should have a girlfriend and I can see quite clearly now that the massive emotions I was feeling were not for Jordan but for the situation.

Anyway, the sublet's fine. My room has a single, tiny window with ancient hinges. It's right above my desk and it's frozen shut. I'm living with a couple (I know, I know), Timothy and Iris, who don't even have a TV, so that's a nice change. Timothy's just finished law school and has decided to take some fine art courses at Concordia, sculpture and stuff. Nice looking, like a klutzy Daniel Day Lewis, if that name means anything to you (do you even go to movies?), except taller and with the inevitable pony-tail. He's downstairs right now banging away at some sheet metal for an installation piece. It's a bit like spiralled wind chimes mixed with a Calder mobile, and all in the key of E minor. Some of his stuff is fine and the rest is bullshit, but, hey, that's the way art is. Iris has a job with a marketing firm downtown. She's fine, nice enough. Westmount, McGill.

Angela Roget was very kind and suggested I come talk to her but I promised myself I would never work for the CBC again. Careers, careers. Just living in Toronto can be a career. Everyone's always working. Even Will. He never stops. I think he made a decision about six months ago to get really serious about his career and he thinks if he acts like a star, people will treat him like one. It's making him a little crazy. The night before I moved he showed up at my place drunk, ranting about what a mistake I was making with my career (what career?). When Jordan came over to help me lift the filing cabinet, Will started baiting him. He'll never forgive Jordan for saying those things about me at that stupid CD release party. I've known Will longer than anyone else but sometimes I don't know what he's doing and I don't think he does either.

You know that beautiful homeless guy in the sheepskin coat that I always used to see outside your office? I didn't see him for about three weeks before I left. I've been thinking about him. Is he still there? Will's convinced he's a performance artist. He always said that nobody that beautiful could end up on the street. Somebody would've saved him.

Anyway, Judith, thanks for suggesting this. I hope you bill OHIP for it.

Kay

◆

Kay Darling,

Your sister sounds like a cross between Cardinal O'Connor and StarHawk. I know she's smart and everything, but why does she try so hard to sound shallow? I called to get your address (you snuck away without giving it to me) and my God but that girl loves to talk. From what I can piece together, she'd just finished reading some Feminist film theorist and she was grilling me about my performance in Salamander Sunrise. I don't know exactly what she was talking about, but it obviously meant a lot to her.

Speaking of which, I ran into that little bit of a waste product you called—I don't know what you called him, I only know what he called you, but we won't go over that again. I went to the wrap party for Liane's film at some warehouse on Spadina and who was hanging with the band (Sleeping Dogs) but Jordan Record Promotions Guy On The Make. Him and his tight-ass Guelph buds in jeans and cowboy boots playing Whiteboy Rock 'n' Roll. WHICH IS SO TIRED. Would you please tell him that he is not from Alabama or Houston, that life is not a beer ad, and that the Dustbowl Depression cowboy troubadour thing does not have anything to do with living in

Toronto in the 90s! I was supposed to meet Bigley there with his new friend from New York (some new happening DJ song-writing friend of Madonna's) but they didn't show. So it wasn't exactly my scene. When I left (after two songs), Jordan was in the hall with some nineteen year old. Little teeny face and big round eyes. Cow Eyes (I'm sure that's what they call her in Wawa or wherever she's from). Anyhow, Cow Eyes was crying, Jordan was drunk, and I was glad to get the hell out of there. I almost felt a twinge of pity for her but then I decided that she's probably as silly and shallow as you, looking for love under rocks and at record release parties (same place if you ask me). "God, it's hard to see someone when you've lost respect for them." I loved that. Just tell me what there was to respect in the first place.

I hope you find this funny. I know I do. And I know you thought you loved him or something but really, Kay, he's Not Your Type. He's only His Type. He's not even Wawa's Type. I don't know why I feel so compelled to tell you all this. I guess it's my way of saying you did the right thing. Reading this over it sounds a bit hostile. But then what's friendship without a bit of hostility? And Feminist film theory?

Agent Pam just called and it looks like I'll be auditioning for M. Tremblay's new family drama at the Centaur. I'll be the droll-older-friend-of-the-artiste-in-waiting yet again. So I'd like to stay chez Kay, unless you're already shacked up with a little moustachioed dépanneur. I can see you now in one of those long raggy sweaters, behind the counter selling wine, smoking and looking bored, which you do so well.

Haven't seen Rodney since he got back, but I saw Dean and he's fine. When I visited him he was sitting up, reading some Jungian thing about yellow and green and telling me he hasn't seen a movie in three weeks. He's calmer now, which is good because he was an absolute drama queen when he first went in the hospital. He said to say hello. Remind me to tell you never to watch a movie with Bigley: he feels compelled to identify every piece of music on the soundtrack.

love Will

♦

4564 rue Clarke
Montreal, Quebec
H2T 2T4

March 18th

Dear Grandy:
Sorry for taking so long to write and sorry that I didn't make it down at Christmas as I had hoped. But I'll see you in August. The move to Montreal went smoothly, which makes six moves in five years. The neighbourhood suits me, though. It's only ten minutes from the mountain and I am walking as much as I can. I'm sure the city has changed since your honeymoon. But the mountain has stayed the same. And the weather. It was -36F yesterday. I don't know how Cartier, Champlain and Co. did it.

Thank you so much for remembering my birthday. The cheque was very generous. I bought a beautiful wool scarf at Ogilvy's to keep me warm. And I was so sorry to hear about Mrs. Underwood. She was always very kind to me and Claire.

Hope your hip is feeling better and I will see you in August.

Love
Kay

Dear Crypto-Conservative Woman,

Just wanked watching a soap. You don't mind me inter-
rupting your celibate lifestyle, do you? (I knew you wouldn't).
Half those boys are fags anyway. I have seen the best bums of my
generation destroyed by soaps. When will there be a soap for
fags? Anyway, I was thinking that letter I sent was a bit bel-
ligerent in places—well, you'd think it was, ya big dyke! Get
over it. I love you. I saw your sister yesterday. She and her
Camay feminists from U of T clomped backstage after the pwyc
matinee to say hello. Kay, they're very sophisticated. They
smoke, they wear workboots, they analyze everything—they
have a very shrewd grasp on the military-industrial-Judeo-
Christian-capitalist conspiracy (but for all their talk, their idea
of a deviant lifestyle is still Graphic Design at OCA). Are you
really going to stay in Montreal? It's boring without you. I'm
bored. No one tells me to shut up.

Dear Kay Again,

Midnight and very cold. Rodney and I just got back from
seeing Wings of Desire and it turns out that I'll be in Montreal
on Friday for the audition so you better count on seeing my pre-
cious white ass. What's your fucking phone number there? If
you don't tell me I'm going to call your mother.

XOXO WW

4564 rue Clarke
Montreal, Quebec
H2T 2T4

March 25th

Dear Claire:
It's late here, too. And thanks for your long letter—you don't know what nightmare scenarios I've been creating for myself these last few days.

To answer your questions, yes, but as you know, the NFB is a tight group, especially in Montreal. And being Suzy-Anglo-girl I'm hardly bilingual, much less Quebecois. They've got their own thing happening. CBC Montreal is, well, CBC Montreal.

No, Davis Brewer is not the main reason but he and his egregious son-of-a-bitch misogynist cowboy bullshit asshole power-plays are a big part of it. When Kenneth was in LA, Davis totally re-cut EMMA'S STORY, the Nickelodeon film I'd worked so hard on, because his ex-partner Kip was the second-unit director which means he shoots all the crap the director can't be bothered to shoot. Of course Kip got the job through Davis who, coincidentally, chose the editor. Get the picture? So when I saw the rough there was all this stupid sentimental second-unit footage that had no right to be there. And when I told Davis there was no way his cut could stand he flipped out and threw one of his little tantrums. "You've got real problems, Kay. You girls are so defensive you think you get the short end of everything. How in love with yourself can you be? You'd be fine if there was someone there to bash your brains out every minute." I am not kidding. That's what he said. And because he won Gryphon some dinky awards, they jizz all over him. But please don't discuss this with anyone; it's a tiny town and you never get work again if you tell tales out of school. A mature adult would simply accept that Davis is a talented director but I'm not a mature adult. And plus I made a vow that I'm not going to say bad things about people anymore.

Not much, but Mom and Dad said they'd help me out if I need it.

Yes, Mom told me about Evelyn. You'd think they would have noticed it before the eighth month. Mom was talking to Aunt Carol and she said they're going to wait a year before they try again. I wanted to call or write a note, but Mom said it's better not to say anything. What do you think?

No, I haven't, but Jordan called me a couple weeks ago drunk and insensible after some film party. One of his new bands, Sleeping Dogs, has a gig at Rockaway at the end of April. So I was stupid and said I'd see him. I do miss odd little things. Like riding on Jordan's motorcycle and having all the other riders wave at you. When you're going out with someone, there are always about six guys you're thinking of having an affair with, but when you're single, it doesn't seem quite as appealing.

I don't know. Realistically, two million dollars, including OFDC, Telefilm and any other various gov't sponsored cash. And in terms of Will being in it, there's really only one male part, and I don't think Will could play Marvin. Speaking of Will, I don't know where he got the idea, but he thinks you're Shirley MacLaine-gone-to-college. And yes, he lives in Will-world and he's a labelist and a show-off and he changes his mind about people about four hundred times a day, but he walks onstage with a charisma all his own and of all the arts-and-entertainment types I know, Will wants to be a star the most and wants to get somewhere, though I don't know if he's sure exactly how he's going to get there. Besides, he gets so excited about himself, you can't help but like him.

By the way, Claire, be a nice lady and don't tell anyone my address or phone number. I really did come here to get the script finished and the idea of people visiting or knowing they can find me distracts me a little. Plus the student-loan sharks are still trying to find me.

Funny coincidence. One of the people I'm living with, Iris Schumacher, says she remembers you from a class at McGill. She cased out my stuff when I was moving in, trying to figure out my background, but when she saw my Mizrahi it was like, oh, she's okay. Soul mates on the strength of a shirt. My room is right above theirs, but so far I haven't heard any schtoinking sounds like the ones that used to reverberate through the house on Euclid. Oh my God, that was a whole year ago. Oh well.

Yeah, I knew Northrop Frye was from Moncton. Grandy knew his mother. I think she lived on Pine or John Street. Somewhere near Grandy. Ask mom, she'd remember. Sorry this is so short. Hasn't Patrick finished that filthy degree yet?

Love
Kay

♦

4564 rue Clarke
Montreal, P.Q.
H2T 2T4

April 2nd. 3 a.m.

Dear Judith:
Oh fuck. Saturday night. Will's here. And he isn't. And I'm

furious. Last night Will was supposed to arrive here at 7. He calls at 8. Apologetic. Meet later. Around 9. Calls at 11. Sorry. Really, really sorry. Can't make it. Change of plans. Call you tomorrow at lunch. Calls the next day at 5:30 pm. Said he had to meet his old NTS teacher and did I want to meet them for a drink later? I got very angry and told him I was through putting up with this bullshit. I know, I know. What can I expect from Will, right? But still, it made me angry because I refused dinner with my cousin whom I haven't seen since I got here. Okay, I'm finally psyched to get some work done when Will arrives here at 8. His old teacher didn't show so Will is determined to cook dinner for me. My roommate Tim comes home. He and Iris have been fighting. So usually Tim just goes downstairs to work because he doesn't want to see Iris. But tonight he hangs around drinking beer watching Will prepare this incredible dinner, this Spanish thing Rodney cooked for my birthday. Will's doing his concerned mature straight act, meanwhile checking Tim out bigtime. We drink a lot of wine. Iris comes home. Tension. She can't stand to see Tim drink. But she likes Will. She tries to charm him but he susses her out in a second and sees right through the cashmere-pearl-button routine because he knows that number cold. After dinner, Will disappears upstairs to use the phone in my room which has rung about a dozen times, all for him. While we're having coffee, Iris finally asks me why I came to Montreal. "Are you from Toronto?" Will asks her, coming back down. Iris demurely shakes her head, no. "Well, people who can't make it in Toronto go to Montreal to learn how to smoke." He pours her more wine. "And when they can't make it in Montreal they go to Moncton and get UI." So then Will starts telling them about this mini-series he did and how it was sold to Channel 4 in the UK and stories about himself and his family and how he hung out with Almodovar in Spain and blah blah blah. Things I've heard a thousand times before. Tim and Iris are sitting there like that's what Stacy did so she wouldn't lose track of them. Incidentally, did you send the pattern and fabric to my mom's or Clarke Street? I talked to your mom this morning and she didn't know. I guess it doesn't matter. As long as it gets here soon. And I like the pale yellow much better than the floral. I'm going to look fat enough as it is, standing next to you and Lisa. I don't need to cover my hips in roses.

Apropos your question, I don't know if Timothy's going to be with me next week, let alone in June, at the rate he's going. He didn't come home last night, Ruth, and I've hardly slept. I told you about this writer who's living with us in John's room now? Well, last night this friend of hers, Will, came to visit, not that we were told he was coming. He's an actor and he's very good-looking, with brown curly hair and rosy cheeks. He was an alien on War of the Worlds up until last year and he's been in a lot of Stratford and Shaw Festival shows. He just finished doing a mini-series with Christopher Reeve about doctors in the Yukon. He also evidently lived with some film director in Spain. For dinner he served us this fantastic paella with a Pinot Noir. He's very funny and articulate; he talks in all these different accents like Dad. Anyway, after we finished the wine, Timothy and Will polished off a bottle of Glenlivet. Then the two of them and Kay went to get more wine and Timothy and Will didn't come back. Kay said she thought they'd be along any time but they weren't so Kay and I stayed up talking and drinking wine until 3 a.m!

You remember Claire Pritchard from Prince Arthur— the one who thought she was a Celtic priestess and was so in love with Jacob she followed him to Israel. I think she ended up working on a kibbutz. Kay's her sister but they're nothing alike. Claire was really outgoing and pleasant to be with, if a bit of a dip. Kay, however, gets on my nerves. She's so condescending, like a mix between Meryl Streep and Miss Crespo—you know, like when she knew you'd seen the movie but hadn't read the book. Most of the time Kay sits at her computer in her ripped jeans, listening to the same tapes over and over again. I can tell she's hardly done any work since she came here, which makes it hard to sympathize with her when she whines about not getting anything done.

Last night, I started talking to her about how worried I am that Timothy hasn't started his bar ads, that he hasn't even looked for an articling position, and how I'm getting a bit fed up with having to pay for everything. I mean at first it was just going to be this one installation project, but now he doesn't want to work and he's preparing a grant proposal to go to a metal-forging course in North Carolina. Kay just sat there on the sofa looking polite and preoccupied as I poured out my heart. I don't even think she was listening.

This morning Kay was making french toast and I kept trying to pretend last night didn't matter when we heard someone bumping into Timothy's sculpture in the basement. I opened the door and this Will and a young man were coming up the stairs. At first I thought he was Will's brother or something. Of course I asked him where Timothy was and apparently Will took him to KOX! Will and this nineteen year old left Timothy there at 3:30 in the morning and no one's seen him since. Please don't tell anyone. Timothy stayed out once before and I told him if he ever did it again it was curtains. Well, he's in for a surprise because he won't find anyone home today. As soon as I found out what happened, I left Montreal and Dad wants me to stay in Magog till Monday morning. As you can imagine, this doesn't help Timothy at all in Dad's eyes. (Speaking of Dad, he wants to buy a new car, so I may buy the Subaru—I finally asked for another raise and got it.)

What I really hate is the worrying, Ruth, when you know he's probably fine but you make up all sorts of terrible scenes in your head. I mean he could've been in a car accident or something. It's just so inconsiderate not to call. You're so lucky to have Alan.

Sorry this letter is so messy. My penmanship was never great and writing in bed certainly doesn't make it any better. I will call you after my fitting. Have you heard from Amy? (I wrote about three months ago and never heard a word.) It will be so great to have everybody there at the wedding. I feel like I haven't seen anybody in ages. After university, you just don't see people anymore. Take care and see you soon.

Love,
Iris

♦

4564 rue Clarke
Montreal, PQ
H2T 2T4

Tuesday. April 5th.

Dear Judith:
Things don't seem to be working out as well as I'd hoped. What did you tell me? Set up a schedule, stick to it. So I've been sitting at my computer for hours at a time, accomplishing nothing. Wandering up and down the mountain. Writing everything except the stupid script. Maybe it's just winter. Probably not. Well, I tried to stick to the schedule but then Will came and everything started to screw up and my romantic notions of Montreal slid away.

To start, Will and Tim stayed out all night. Will showed up again on Saturday afternoon with some kid named Kevin. "Oh, is that your brother?" Iris asks Will. "Yeah," I felt like saying. "And that thing your cat's playing with is his little brother's butt plug." Where do these girls come from? Didn't anyone ever tell Iris anything? She couldn't understand how Will could leave Tim alone in any bar, let alone a gay bar. "And you just left him there?" Like the guy's suddenly defenceless in a room full of fags. Of course Will left him there. Beauty may be important and Tim may be cute, but a straight guy's a straight guy. Except when they're not, but Tim is. He's just trying to find something that interests him. But Iris doesn't quite seem to catch on to any of this. She is the original straight girl who doesn't know anything about what's going on in the world and still thinks that men will protect you and you can live happily ever after. Leave it to Will to fuck up a nice girl's value system. So Tim never did show up again that weekend. He just deserted. Iris retreated to her dad's house in the townships so she didn't even know if Tim was here or not, but every hour or so someone called and hung up when the machine came on. Tim finally arrived home Monday at lunch. When Iris got home after work things were horribly tense so I went out to dinner with my cousin, finally. I came back at midnight to find Iris sitting at my desk. She couldn't sleep. Tim told her he spent the weekend at a friend's but she didn't believe him. "Why didn't he call? Why wouldn't he call? It doesn't make any sense." She told me that they had decided to break up which translates into: Find a new place to live.

And for the first time in three months I started crying, right in front of fatty Iris. Now I've been a little nasty about Iris because of her snotty attitudes and poor little rich girl complaints, but when she sat there with her big treacherous cow eyes all swollen and red I couldn't think of a thing to say. On Saturday she told me that she and Tim hadn't been sleeping together for a long time. And now, instead of becoming a corporate lawyer, Tim wants to move to Prague to be a sculptor. This is pretty difficult for Iris because her oldest friend's getting married in June and instead of Iris getting engaged herself, her boyfriend of four years has dumped her. Or she's dumped him. It doesn't matter. It was so frighteningly predictable, though. That's what's scary. That's why I cried. It seemed like everyone else could see it except her. Iris should have known. But she didn't want to know. She believes her own marketing. She just assumes things are what she thinks they are. She takes things, accepting their mere presence as gifts tagged for her. She has an odd kind of independence that depends on strategically placed blind spots. Iris didn't want to know and Tim didn't want to talk about it and both of them wanted to blame each other.

So why does it make me mad? Because I have to move again. The idea of piling up all my books and disks and shoes and socks and dragging them across the city exhausts me. I thought that maybe in Montreal I'd be able to get everything to slow down a little, just for a minute, just so I could get my lands in order. At least Iris knows what she wants. I'm not the Little Miss Big City Smarty Pants I thought I was, coming to Montreal to relax, finish some writing, and lose all the craziness. Have I always been like this? Will I always be like this? If only self-obsession were a viable way of life, then I could have a wonderful career. No wonder Davis freaked on me. I'm a nightmare because I try to control everything. But Davis was an asshole. This is really stupid, isn't it? I spend half my life trying to cover up all this emotional messiness and the other half trying to explain it away. I should have just stuck to the schedule.

I just can't believe I have to move, though. Fucking Will, on top of all this, just before he left, Dean called him and told him that he got his Canada Council Project Grant. Five grand to go see plays in New York, with a promise to do a play at the

Tarragon which I think the Tarragon already agreed to do anyway. I remember when I got up at six to type that goddamned proposal for him which he threw together in one sloppy afternoon so he could courier it to Ottawa in time: "I feel I have a lot to offer both as an actor and writer to Canada …" Bigtime blah blah blah. I can't believe it. That's so fucking like Will to get it, too. What amazes me is the way he has of disrupting everyone else's life with careless stunts, while winning consistently in his own.

I hate how stupid and frantic I sound in this letter. Do you know I just debated with myself for three minutes about doing a spell check? I'm sick of spell checks.

Kay

♦

6:00 p.m.
7 April 91

Back in T.O.

Hello Sister.

I didn't get the Tremblay part—which I didn't want anyway! But I got my grant money so what do I care? And it looks like R&J again at Stratford this summer. Et tu, Kathleen? Have you got your shit together yet? Or are you sinking deeper into whatever it is you're sinking into? Are you still a total wreck like I've told everyone here?

BFD. Get over it. Now. Because while you're looking around the Plateau for a life, picking away at the world with your little Catholic-girl code of ethics, making out your little lists, I've been doing you mondo favours here in the city where it happens. I schmoozed who out to lunch? Davis "Berlin Film Festival" Brewer who, as it happens, has his little pinky on the pulse of Forest Hill, Hollywood, the Kremlin, and the Dow Jones Industrial Average. We did not, repeat not, talk about you so relax, Miss Thing. Not by name anyway. My Spidey-sense tells me he feels RIGHT BAD about what happened. He hinted that McKeen and Angela at CBC need a script editor for that new media-watchdog show "Agenda" and the hinting is you. It's posted within the CBC so get to it.

Dean's fine. He's out of the hospital and goes to physio at Mt. Sinai Tues. and Thurs. nites. No more soccer. And my best to Timothy, who incidentally is definitely not a Die. You just hate pony-tails.

So, my little highwire act, kick butt or move to Moncton.

Will

♦

April 12th, 1991

Kay Pritchard
4564 rue Clarke
Montreal, PQ
H2T 2T4

Angela Roget
CBC
Station A
Toronto, Ontario
M5W 1E6

Dear Angela:
I am sending you my résumé in response to the CBC posting for the position of script editor for AGENDA.

Will

I'M ON THE STAIRS, on my way out, house music thump thump thump in the stairwell. There's Dean downstairs. Red baseball cap. Jeans. Blue plaid shirt. Standing in the doorway, looking in at the dance floor, holding a beer bottle, doing the dinky little dance you do in bars. Working the working-class aesthetic.

—Hey Willy Weston, he says, seeing me. You're getting right snobby, eh? Too much of a star to say hello?

—How are you, Dean? Growing a beard again?

—I'm stupid.

He's looking in at someone. He looks back at me.

—You were in my dream the other night.

—How'd I look, okay?

—Of course. Actually, you looked better. You had a haircut.

Dean's staring at the young man in the shirt and tie, for-get-his-name, Dean already introduced me to him. Dean's been dating them for years but it never works. The type who write Straight-Acting in the personals.

—He's so perfect, Dean says. And the stupid part is I still love them.

—Of course you do. And they still fuck you over.

—Do you like him?

—Of course. I love charming boys with nice manners.

Faux private-school boys.

—This one's the worst, Dean says, wincing. Stoned every night. And a thief. But I'm such a sucker for affection. He grabs my balls and whispers in my ear and I'm putty in his hands. He's been at my house for a week. Where's Stephano?

—At the bar, I say, buttoning my coat. I'll be right back.

I pat Dean on his shoulder and turn as someone screams my name. It's Bigley, model slash actor read waiter, with affected accent, English because he spent a year there, these guys never learn.

—Will! he says. My God, where have you been? We haven't seen you.

He raises his eyebrows, stretching his face. He's so loud, so actorly.

—What have you been doing?
—New York, I say.
—Really? How wonderful. What were you doing there?
—Acting.
—Oh, that's good. You look great.

He doesn't take his eyes from my face, smiling like there's something I'll be hearing about later.

—Come by and have a drink sometime, he adds and wanders off.

My God, it's like everyone thinks you have AIDS the minute they haven't seen you for two weeks. And he must know about New York. Dean beside me still doing the dinky dance. Same all over the world. In New York, Italy, Japan, clubs filled with men in jeans and white T-shirts, dancing, drinking, and loud the music, everyone going home with ringing in their ears.

Outside cold winter air, foolish climate, bad for your skin. Remember frostbite when I was ten walking home from school, brittle skin peeling. Mom rubbing cream into my ears, everyone would see the marks. I took the injury personally, of course. Where's a cab, busiest time of year, isn't it? Snowy sidewalk, salt stains creeping over the toes of my shoes. I look up at the clean edges into the sky of the buildings downtown, little windows with people within, office parties, Christmas parties … There's a cab.

—Carlton and Mutual, please.

Toes cold. Hope Kay is waiting inside, knows better than to stand like a whore in kid leather boots. Remember when Mom envied their fur coats, thought they'd appropriated part of her world, until she realized, my God if anyone needs a fur coat they do. And Kay still at work. Disgraceful. Doing what till midnight on the Friday before Christmas? Like *A Christmas Carol. A Christmas Kay*, woman of situations. Remember today the flight attendant telling me he works twenty-four hours at a time over Christmas. A little mini-crush on him for a minute. Gave us free drinks. Wanted my phone number. Cute but intensely lost up there in the air, wandering around, you never come down. Except to Barbados or Barbuda or Bimini … Along the street three trannie-hookers. I know them all. Don't think my parents raised me to know trannie-hookers. Taxi driver speeding through the yellow light and there's Kay on the corner breathing cold breaths. I tell the driver we're picking that woman up—does he think she's working? No, they're out here enough—and he swings a U-turn to her side of the street.

Kay waves, smiling to see me, rosy cheeks, her hair different. She looks into the cab, puzzling, searching for another person, then pulls the door open.

—So where is he? she says, bundling into the back seat, leaning over to kiss me.

I take her hand.

—Where is this guy? Where's the much-heralded Stephano?

—What a great haircut, I say. You look fab. Everyone will want to fuck you.

—Where is he? she says, taking her hand away, oh, she has to blow her nose.

I love it when she's skanky.

—Kathleen, really. Working till midnight the Friday before Christmas. Who do you think you are?

—Is he coming for sure?

—He's already there.

—I thought he might be too tired.

—Stephano miss a party? You obviously haven't met him.

—My God I feel like I know him already. You haven't stopped talking about him.

—How often am I excited about a man, Kay? It's been years.

—I know, I know. How long you in town?

—Just till tomorrow.

—Me too. You going home for Christmas?

—Yeah.

—With Stephano?

—Yeah, Mom said to bring him. They want to meet him.

—That's a switch.

—They think it's okay now that I'm such a star. A star in New York. A star in New York and a fag in North Bay.

—Whatever happened to Patsy Gallant?

Kay smiling, in a good mood. Oh, we like this. Kay enjoying herself.

—What have you been doing? I say. Writing your script?

—No, I've been working.

—Oh my God. The CBC. How is it? How's Angie-baby?

—Good. She's good. I like it. It's fine.

—Have you finished your script yet?

—Haven't had any time.

—Well, you'd better hurry. I'm writing one. I showed it to a producer who really liked it. The shit I saw in New York, I can fucking come up with something better.

—What is it, a play or a screenplay?

—It's just a script, Kay.

—What's it about?

—It's about you. It's about you. It's about a little uptight straight white girl who if she had any sense at all would be a dyke but she's not, so she settles for being the biggest fag-hag in the greater Metropolitan Toronto area.

—Oh. I think I've read it. *The Bell Jar.* She dies in the end.

—Right. But she's not going to in mine. I'm going to drag her through every greasy grimy detail of modern life.

Kay pensive a moment.

—It's not really about me, is it, Will?

—Totally. It's the first fag-hag epic.

—I deny that, she says. I'm not a fag-hag. Fag-hags want to fuck fags.

—Except in my script you're successful.

Kay laughs, shakes her head. I bump over and buss her ear.

—Ow, she says. Get off. I have a bruise there.

—Huh? How'd you get a bruise there?

—I don't know how, but it hurts.

—Oh, Kay. Don't be so much like yourself.

She wipes at her ear with her fingers.

—You've got a nerve saying that to someone.

—Well, you know, Kay, I almost got you this Christmas present in New York. This skirt that I knew you'd look absolutely fabulous in, but I knew you'd never wear it because you never wear anything too tight or above your knee.

—Oh, Will. I would've worn it.

—No, you wouldn't.

—What's it made out of?

—I don't know. It's cheap sexy, but cheap sexy's still sexy. Very high waisted.

—So why are you telling me this? So I'll say I would've hated it and let you off the hook. Forget it. I'd wear it.

—Good. Because I bought it for you. And that's why you have to pay for the cab.

Kay leaning into the front seat.

—You're always late, she says, paying the driver. And you never have any money. It's pathetic.

Nervous kids in the line-up waiting for the bouncer to let them in, that's pathetic. Saint Peter at the gate. I show my stamp and drag Kay in behind me. Blasé coat-check girl collecting coats, stuffing scarfs and mittens in sleeves. Dry bleached hair switching back and forth across her face. Kay checks her pockets before throwing her coat across the counter. She takes the small brass disc from the girl, puts it in her pants pocket and leans against the wall, waiting for me.

—Will, she says, is Rodney here?

—He just left.

—Oh.

—He has a meeting tomorrow.

—On Saturday?

—I know.

—Oh, Will, Kay says. Remind me to call Angela, would you?

At the top of the stairs someone of indeterminate gender in gold wig and red sparkle gown. Kay stops beside her, staring, where does she think she is—the Louvre? Gold wig whispering something to Kay and I know that voice, it's Pia Mess, drag queen extraordinaire from Montreal. Kay laughs and Pia flips her long black fingers at me in a oh-hello-how-are-you-how-do-you-like-my-pedestal kind of way. Sister, you look amazing. Don't know if you're as fucked-up as people say, but at least you look fabulous doing it. Might as well. Fucked-up in an innocent kind of way really. Wonder where all the drag queens go. To be an ageing fag, sure, but an ageing drag queen? What happened to Donna Matrix anyway? Where did she go? Where will Pia be when she's fifty?

Stephano on the other side of the room standing alone beside the enormous picture window. His dark curly hair swept back from his face, his dark skin and straight nose, long-lashed eyes, looking as if he's just fallen from the ceiling of the Sistine Chapel. He's playing with the frost on the inside of the window, moving it back and forth, making a little see-through space. I point him out to Kay. She's already looking at him.

—Oh my, Kay says, surprised she's surprised. Is that him? He's incredibly cute, Will.

—I don't think cute is the word, Mary. I think it's god-like.

—He really does look like Joe Dallesandro.

—I know. I can't stand it. It's a bit of a cliché except that he's so totally, totally, totally sexy. He's like one of the two or three best-looking individuals I've seen in my life.

—Claire will love him. He's gorgeous.

—Just imagine how sexy God must be.

Kay laughs her deep unreserved laugh. It sounds much bigger than she is. That place where her laughter is.

—Kathleen Pritchard, I'd like you to meet Stephano Giovanni Sissmondo.

Hates it when you call her Kathleen. She extends her hand.

Stephano smiles, dimples.

—Ullo.

Perfect wrinkles.

—*Buena sera*.

—*Buena sera*.

Stephano asks Kay if she'd like something to drink.

—I can get something, Kay says.

—No problem, Stephano says.

—*Noah Problemo*, I say. *Donna ya lova tha, Kay? Donna it jussa maka-ya melt?*

—Scotch? Stephano asks me, touching my hand and kissing me lightly.

Kissed in front of Kay before? Kay turns to me when he's gone.

—Okay, she says, so tell me.

—Tell you what?

—Tell me all about it. Tell me how wonderful he is.

—He *is* wonderful, I say. I love him. I'm a teenager on a bus. I can't shut up about it. I'm on a bus. It's true, Kay. I mean just look at him. We've been together every day for two and a half months and I still love him. I mean, usually after about six weeks I'm completely bored and I get a bit itchy. But with Steph it's different. I mean he has his own career and his paintings are fantastic and he's smart. So I thought, why not? When I met him, I thought, like why not? I mean, if someone's going to love me, I better start to learn to love them back, right? I just decided why not forget all of the stupid pride and let myself be in love? I've never done it before. At least not *with* anyone. Who loved me back, I mean. Five years ago I would have denied this could even happen. And wait until you see his paintings. You'll die. You will die. They're magnificent.

—This is the same Will who said that sex with the same person for more than two weeks was boring?

—I was wrong. I was wrong wrong wrong. Thank God, I was wrong. But I mean look at him, Kay. It's like having my own private David sculpture.

Stephano pushing his hips onto the brass rail along the edge of the bar, calling to the bartender. Only his toes touch the floor. One hand on the bar, the other sweeping back and forth behind him, searching for a chair. He's like a hundred men distilled into one sweet thing. How can Kay stand to go out with those skinny guys?

—What's his work like? Kay says.

And I tell about the quarter-page Steph got in the New York Times and that the SteinGladstone Gallery ran a show on American Machismo and Steph did this series called "Over Four Billion Serviced" of giant, giant canvases, eight by sevens and twelve by nines, very thick oils, garish colours, genitals and eyeballs and sexual figures, very figurative black bulls, like ancient cave paintings.

—You should see them, I say. They're amazing. Absolutely amazing. My God, people think he's going to be really big, Kay. I want him to have a show here, but his agent doesn't want him to. He shows only in New York and Milan. *Milano.*

—How much are they?

—Oh, fuck, I don't know. Really expensive. His next show is called "Hunter or Dancer."

—Oh Will, Kay says, there's Claire and Patrick. I'm just going to go say hi.

—Kay?

—Yeah.

—Call Angela.

Kay smiles, making her way through the crowd. Claire, little-sister syndrome, but looking glam tonight, the blonde babe in the velvet dress, flipping her hair, she has her own thing happening, hangs with all the pretty feminists. Her man beside her, Patrick, waxing polemic, very cute but has that yes-you-may-have-an-opinion-but-I-have-a-PhD way of listening which must piss Kay off. Voice in my ear.

—Who *is* that man?

Bigley again, with a vodka tonic and a cigarette, standing with Dean, all his weight on one leg. Bigley wearing an "outfit," must be back in his chi-chi downtown restaurant, all those trendy waiter boys splurging on clothes, marking time. Bigley talking to me because he thinks I'm going to be famous. Half these people sitting around waiting for me to be famous, other half waiting for me to fuck up. So they can say they know me, or knew me and hated me even before I was famous. Remember Dean said Bigley has the biggest schlong in the city. Dean the size queen claims he's seen every famous dick in Ontario. Bigley smiling again like he's a bit too eager to see me, his eyes a little wider than normal. He pushes back his hair, his cigarette still in his hand, shifts his weight to his other leg.

—Will Weston, he says, *Who* is that man at the bar?

Offers me a cigarette, Camels, no thanks, terrible for you, big warning on the pack: Smoking during pregnancy can harm the baby. When did Mom start? When Peter Jackson had that contest trip to Hawaii. Hawaii very big in the seventies.

—Stephano, I say.

—Stephano who?

—Stephano Giovanni Sissmondo.

—Stephano *Sissmondo*?

—*Si.*

Bigley looks at me very blasé, blasé.

—How do you know him? I mean, what does he do?

Bigley doesn't know Steph, hasn't heard of him, can't read him.

—He's working on a screenplay, I say.

—No, I mean what's he really do?

—He's a scriptwriter.

—A real scriptwriter?

—No, Bigley, he's a fictional one. I wrote him, actually. In fact, I wrote him into this party scene. Don't you like his outfit?

—Ha ha. We all can't be as funny as you, Will. What kind of scripts has he written? Like for TV you mean?

—*Dangerous Liaisons*.

—The movie?

Bigley slaps his hand against his chest. Dean smiling.

—Well, I *loved* it. I saw it in Miami.

Bigley the place-dropper. That reminds me of this café in Bermuda ... When I was working in Provence ... We met this gorgeous woman in the Napa valley ... Cindy Crawford at La Guardia, London Paris Rome Munich ... Bigley turns back to me.

—I spent the whole film staring at his hairline. What's he working on now?

—He's got a deal with Paramount. A silence contract till the star signs.

Bigley looks over at Stephano again, lifts his glass to finish his vodka tonic.

—*Dangerous Liaisons*, he says, crunching the ice with his back teeth. That was so smart. How did he come up with that?

—He stole it.

—Really? You mean like from another writer?

—Yeah. The guy who wrote *Cyrano*. Rostand.

—Really? It was in French, wasn't it?

Bigley checks his drink for ice one more time.

—You guys want another drink?

Dean thanks him, no.

—Will?

—No thanks. Goodnight, Desdemona.

—Who?

Oh, please. Bigley smiles and goes. Dean looks at me.

—You are evil, he says, rubbing my shoulder.

Dean always nice to these Bigleys. Indulges them. You never know, he says. One of them might do something really good. Dean always hugging us. He's going to the dance floor again, he says, looking for his boy, forget his name.

Stephano at the bar, talking to Kay and Claire, charming, he's standing like a matador, one foot aimed off the ankle of the other, sees me and holds up a finger. One minute. Impatient. He loves the high, just loves the high, keening intensity, likes heights, too. Looking out the window on the flight in. He's whispering to Claire now, grinning, his mouth opening wide to laugh. White teeth. He walks down the hall to the bathroom and I follow the squaring of his shoulders, the beautiful back, sweet man in my bed tonight, can't keep my hands off him and I'm a teenager on a bus again. The empty bathroom, fluorescent lights and Stephano bending down and rounding up small piles of powder along the counter. His clever hands. So meticulous, cleaning them of paint, yet no dry rough skin, thin silver band on his right hand. He inspects his thumb-nail for a second, like it's too long or too dirty, then deftly spreads the powder back and forth, back and forth till there are four lines no longer than two inches. Quiet, concentrating. His great Roman nose inhales. Throwing back his head, twitching his nose slightly, rubbing it. Passing me the red-and-white straw.

—It's not bad, he says. As good as any of the crap in New York.

It'sa nada baad. Os goood as any a tha craap ina New Yoork.

I lean down and do a line and the blow charging behind my eyes blinking a series of instant snapshots: the left side of Stephano's face, the door edge framed by the ceiling corners, the grey spot in my finger, the white edge of my shirt-cuffs, the reflection sparkling in the faucet ... Stephano's hands wiping the tip of his nose and he looks at me smiling, a job well done, comrade.

Out of the bathroom and talking in the corridor, Kay's erstwhile beau, dude-meister and bonehead, Jordan Goodnight, chatting up some 24-Hour model babes. His straight-boy bravado sort of amusing, because you think he's got a bullshit attitude about himself, but not so much anymore. He's nice, that's the thing. Treats everybody the same. He's got one of his pals with him, another of the inexhaustible supply of rock-boy sidekicks. This one a cute goofy chap, a rebel in a Roots jacket, pimple on his chin, but a gold Ethiopian hat on his head. What must Kay think, seeing Jordan at ease here with his little Barbie No-Minds? Thank God she walked out of the Rivoli that night when she did. Who'd want to spend the rest of their life pretending to like stupid rock bands?

Jordan, quiet, peeling the label from his beer bottle, takes a swig, sees me and it's like what-a-surprise-to-see-you-here. God they all think they're Tom Waits.

—Will, Jordan says in his little surfer-voice.

It's sort of ironic, I guess, except it isn't. He raises his beer bottle in a toast to me and smiles. Dimples, a nice smile and I see where he'd be a good fuck. A good dirty fuck. But there's lots of those out there. Though didn't Kay say cool boys are lousy lays? Always drunk.

—This is Henley, Jordan says, introducing the sidekick, one of the Sleeping Dogs, I see.

Henley very cute but very drunk, full of beer, the rock boys' answer to anorexia. Got a very Rob Lowe thing happening, but the Ethiopian hat, they were a bad idea even when they were hip.

—Whoa, Henley says, you can bet Henley says whoa a lot, catching sight of another chick.

He blows his bangs out of his face and flicks his head at Jordan, a check-it-out gesture. Then he smiles, cutie-boy smile, and taps his beer bottle against his front teeth, letting the world get a good look at him. These boys, always thinking about the next chippy, flashing smiles, playing with their need to be desired. God, I can see the whole thing now. One good song and he keeps his hair and in three years it's "Sometimes it's the lyrics first and sometimes it's the music. But we don't care if we sell a million records, we just want to make a great album. I mean, do you know what we're doing to the environment?" And the sad truth is a lot of fags would go crazy for him. Like the Gasworks boys, the sweet street-trash who go cruising after the bars close. Oh well. There it is.

—Are you going to the speak? Jordan asks.

—Which one?

—The new one, on Richmond. The Cantina. Eric's organizing it.

Eric? Oh, please. Jordan's sole gay-friend, Eric so cool he barely even knows any fags. Little Warhol wanna-be polaroids everything. The straight boys' Joe Alternative. An effort of sorts, yet these boys annoy me. What scene are they looking for? Looking to be at the centre of something, the hub of downtown, a scene, a groover's habitat, a hinterland's who's who.

—So you're going to a speak? I ask.

—Oh yeah. Kay here?

—At the bar, I say, and walk on by.

I'm too serious now, maudlin, coked-out already. Can't be bothered. Slips me into hypercritical space. The little imbalances going on in my ears, I'm better off in open spaces because the back of my head is opening up. *Naatsa baad*? Stardust. Maybe if I dance. Out of the hallway. Sweat. Smell. Slippery floor. The boom boom bass, house music, and Pia Mess tango queen among all the hunter dancers. Prima donna supreme. Work, Miss Honey, work.

Have another pop-over, froggy. A scotch before last call but better watch it, better watch it, right? Addictive personality, obsessive behaviour, a need to entertain. Children of alcoholics.

If I'm not careful I'll end up in LA, fit right in. Of course I'll be successful. Upstairs bar less crowded all the dinkerooneys downstairs. Someone waving at me from a table, can't see who—oh, Michael Podowinski, self-important bit actor, met him at Stratford. Benvolio. One of those guys who pegs you down, sits beside you, and for the next half hour tells you about all the wonderful things that almost happen to him. Look how drunk he is. His eyes too fucked-up to focus. Is he gay? I don't even know if he's gay. He probably doesn't know. You watch, he'll be thirty-three and finally come out with a vengeance, a born-again fag, thinking he's the only man in history to be tempted by one of his own sex, then peg you down and lecture you on the beautiful poetry of gay life and want to get married, collect antiques and have a cat. He's sitting with all the ageing cool waitresses. Only so long you can be a cool waitress. Dangerously ageing. These people, some of these people, God, it's Gilligan's Island. Some of these people never leave. Waiting around for their lives to happen. Get on with it. So many of these people, they don't want to do anything, they just want to be stars. Coke, man. Twenty minutes of fun and then you turn into a prick. But coming home, coming home always more exciting than getting home.

Upstairs, third floor, abandoned bar, what time is it, and there's Kay all alone, home alone, like her gig as a ghost walking the streets of Montreal. She's half-sitting on a bar stool, writing something into her filofax, her right hand holding a wine glass by her cheek. Jordan so foolish to have acted the little cool-boy with Kay, not noticing her, as if no one would notice her, so crazy because try looking at Kay from the left when she doesn't know you're looking, and, wham, if she dressed a bit better, she'd be one of those fabulous don't-fuck-with-me babes. I sneak over and look into her filofax which I didn't notice her having before or did I?

—Hello, darling, she says.

—I'm so sick of Elvis.

—Which one?

—All of them. Kay, honey, what are you doing being serious? And Kay?

—What?

—Call Angela.

—Oh, fuck.

—You mean you didn't call her?

—No, I meant to tell Claire that I'd pick her up tomorrow morning.

—Did she go?

—Yeah. About half an hour ago.

—God, you're as good as they get, Mary. You're a right-on sister. You're the limit, the absolute limit.

—Yeah? Oh, I like this song.

—Thank God I know you. You're my best girlfriend. And I just hate the idea of some other fag having this conversation.

—Couldn't happen.

I lean down and take a sip from Kay's red wine. All the cigarette smoke's making my eyes ache. Kay smoking like at York.

—Kay?

—Yeah.

—Are you ever going to have babies?

—Tons, she says, looking up from her filofax.

Try to read what she's writing, still can't read it. Notes in Kay's head. Kind of scary.

—Tons of babies, she says. And a ranch. And a hot tub. And a husband named Tyler. And then I'm going to kill myself.

—At least you get a ranch. Sylvia only got a couple of poems.

—*Will*, she says, standing up. You smell just like my Uncle Bert. How much have you had?

—I've had enough to be Uncle Bert. What're you doing? You going? Why?

—It's almost one-thirty.

—It is?

I pick up Kay's wrist and look at her watch. That the right time? I guess I've been living in party time, haven't been paying attention with all the faces and everyone being together.

—Are you guys staying? Kay says.

—I think so. Are you going to the speak?

Kay shakes her head are-you-crazy?

—Where's Stephano?

—I don't know where he is right now. I think he's dancing.

—Claire and I had a little talk with him. He's lovely. Claire thought he was amazing.

—When? Just after you got here?

—Yeah.

—What time's your flight tomorrow?

—Eleven.

—Are you staying for New Year's?

Kay nods.

—Well, Kay, see you next year.

She nods again and pulls a little box out of her pocket. It's wrapped in blue cloth, with pink ribbon. A little note fastened on top with a tiny kilt pin:

To Will
Do not open until Christmas
And then only for a little while
Love Kay

With a wave of the hand and a little bend-down-here's-a-hug, Kay makes her way through the drunk party-makers and slips down the stairwell before I even have a chance to tease her if she's getting laid or not. Not that she'd tell. She never tells anyone anymore. Not even long-distance.

I sit at the bar and undo the pin and in the box is a little pink triangle and I laugh because it's my first and last earring. Remember the day I arrived in Toronto to go to university, terrified nineteen year old, the future all in front of me like someone else's road, longest street in the world. An hour after I got off the bus I went to have my ear pierced. Some shop, black leather accessories hanging from chains. Zippers, loops, whips, and a woman in a ratty black dress and blue lipstick. She took me to the back room, iced my ear and jammed a needle through my ear lobe. The things you do. Triangle, insect and anarchy symbol the only earrings to choose from. Bitter old clone sitting behind the desk. Paid twenty-five dollars and walked out a new man, right into Yonge Street, hundreds of people drifting along the sidewalks selling or buying affordable glamour, sunglasses, drugs, video games, sex. A skinny kid with a sore ear gawking his way down Yonge Street. How long did I have it? A month, two months. Till one night sitting at the back of a club, stoned, drunk from whiskey sours, my ear infected, sending painful jabs down the side of my neck. Staring at a little tear in the wallpaper, to the left of me. If I could keep still for just a minute my stomach might settle. "Are you all right?" he asked me, and I slowly turned my head to avoid my hurting ear. A man wearing tight black pants, a Raiders T-shirt, and cowboy boots. The kind of guy I longed for in North Bay, round tight biceps, the beautiful chest, clean-shaven, your friend's older brother. "You don't look very well. Maybe you'd like to go for a walk?" He held out his hand and I took it. Little cuts in his fingers. I'm a chef, he told me. He began to talk, telling me about when he arrived in Toronto. He said hello to passing men and later told me who they were, how he knew them, what they did. We wandered through what I later realized was the gay ghetto, Church-Wellesley-Second Cup, walked for blocks, stopping for a coffee in a donut shop. When we returned to the street, Rodney hailed a cab, and my stomach turned once more, rejecting both the coffee and the thought of being left alone. Surely he wanted something more than a walk. It never occurred to me that he might see me as the slightly drunk, naïve idiot I was and I got into his cab anyway. A week later I moved into his apartment. When I went back to York to collect my stuff, I went to Kay's room in Vanier to take out my earring. Remember staring at Kay's Blondie poster, listening to "Tainted Love" over and over, as eighteen-year-old Kay with her asymmetrical, Phil Oakey haircut disinfected my ear, completely disgusting. I couldn't touch it for a week. Six years ago, York was. Seven. Me and Kay sitting in the library playing Fuck or Die. And me and Rodney. That June when half the city undressed, in shirts and shorts. All those new shiny bodies, new boys in town and Rodney expecting nothing less, so why waste it? I was one of them.

Rodney the sensible activist now. Personnel administrator. Connections with wealthy straight people, organizes events, gets publicity, donations. Cooks for the Every Dyke a Hero Dinner. But also stinky work, like renovating the community centre. Rodney forty-two years old now and living with a series of fucked-up innocent young fags-on-the-run. More renovation. Saint Rodney, really. Must have dinner with him, Steph and I. Must call him Christmas Day. Rodney's crazy mother and father. Tragic, tragic. So what else is new? Tired now. Close my eyes and feel like I'm still on the plane, turbulence, the bumpy landing. Some people still up in the air, arriving home, their flights delayed. North America. All the people right now in their different time zones. Why'd I think of that? Oh yeah, the flight attendant. God, everything always beginning. Always fucking beginning. Everything always beginning all over again.

—Bigley was looking for me?

—Yeah, they couldn't find you. I said maybe you'd gone to the speak. Do you want to go?

—Are you going now?

—Yeah, dude.

We arrive, Jordan and I, and two big guys guard the line-up outside, another guy selling hot dogs. Jordan walks past the line-up, of course, and pulls out his card. Record executive. Almost. They wave us in, up the stairs. Twenty bucks gets you in the door and two beer at the bar. The Cantina an old dress factory of three rooms with a bar in one, DJ in another, can't see what's in the third. In front are dancers, flitting around one another. People on sofas talking. Light from a lamp-post outside drifts in, a cool quiet atmosphere. A young girl in a feather dress asking her friend where to go for breakfast. Groovers on X will stay to watch the sun rise. Feel old when you see these kids. Starting to feel like why-did-I-come-this-is-stupid when a camera flashes and there he is in the next room, I see Stephano again not twenty feet in front of me and he salutes me happily, drunkenly, as if I haven't just panicked that I lost him forever on our first night back; he smiles as if everything's fine, and really it is, it's a dream, and the earring in my pocket, I'm on my way over to whisper in his ear what I want to do to him later and I know I'm finally in my future, and yesterday and tomorrow mix in one lovely moment on my way across the room.

Kay Again

IT WAS JUST AFTER five o'clock on the slushy and cold Tuesday evening of February 18th, 1992. Kay Pritchard stood in the middle booth of the triple telephones at the southwest corner of Bloor Street and Avenue Road talking on a phone. She wore a camel-hair overcoat of her father's—she'd just had the sleeves darned and the plastic buttons replaced with horn—black Beatle boots, double-knit black pants, a tan-coloured turtleneck sweater (hand-knit by her grandmother), a three-button sports jacket, and draped around her auburn hair, a red-and-yellow plaid wool scarf.

Face down on the pay phone's square top lay the Arts Section of that day's *Globe and Mail* and the March issue of *Toronto Life*. On the back cover of the magazine, over a glossy advertisement for Maybelline New Active Wear Make-up— "Make-up That Can Face Anything"—Kay had been quickly writing with a black felt-tip pen as she talked.

"So what is it, stress child?" the man on the phone asked. "What are you running away from this time?"

"I want to quit."

"Why?"

"I'm sick of it. It's so—"

"Oh, Cinderella, it's a great job. You can't quit a job every time you get bored."

"It's not boredom, Will."

"Kay, do you know what happens when you die?"

There was a pause before Kay responded. "What?"

"They write an obituary and it's printed in the paper. And

they list all the things you've accomplished, not all the men you've loved or all the principled decisions you've made. Get it? What are they going to write? 'She found a nice one-bedroom apartment in Toronto?' Or 'She quit her first job at the age of seventeen and—'"

"Shut up, Will."

"Sure." He waited. "Look, it happens to everyone. Everybody gets bad press. That's what critics do."

"It's not criticism, Will. It was just nasty. That guy knew what he was going to say even before he saw the show."

"It's only the *Globe*."

"Only the *Globe*? Like it only has a circulation of about four hundred thousand."

"Yeah, but nobody reads the Arts Section."

"Nobody except the whole industry."

"Well, come on, Kay. What do you guys expect when you're out there slamming everybody? That they're going to want to be your friend?"

"We're hardly slamming everybody."

"And who was that guy who wouldn't shut up about Glooscap? Where did you find him? Why didn't you just cut him out of the show?"

Kay looked up from her writing. "I don't know, Will. It's just so—oh fuck."

"What?"

"Nuns. Across the street. I don't want to see nuns. It's bad luck."

"Hey, have you finished your script yet?"

"No."

"Well, finish it and then you'll be fabulously wealthy and successful and you won't care about stupid TV shows. Or nuns. Because you're just putting it off."

"I'm not putting it off. I haven't had a moment to—"

"Pam thought it sounded great."

"Will. Don't you—I don't want people to know that I'm working on a scr—"

"Hold on, sweetie. I've got another call."

"Okay, I'm hanging up."

"No, I'll be right back."

"I'm hanging up."

"No, you're not and you're not quitting your job."

Kay heard the phone click. She waited. She turned around to see where the nuns had gone, but it was darker now and harder to see past her reflection in the glass. A few feet away a bicycle courier waited for his light to change. Kay watched him cheat into the intersection, jerking and jockeying to stay balanced on his pedals. The light changed, the courier zig-zagged toward Yonge Street, the rest of the traffic chased after him, and Kay swung around and banged the receiver down.

She wrote a few more lines on the back of the magazine before stopping to re-read the whole page. She stood there a moment, as if rendered inert, then, with a jolt of purpose, she took off her right-hand glove, took two quarters from her pants pocket and fed one into the pay phone. She dialed. After the first ring a woman's voice answered.

"Hello?"

"What are you doing?"

"Oh, hi, Kay. Nothing. I'm just typing this thing for Tasha and kind of working on an essay. Where are you?"

"I'm waiting to see Judith in about fifteen minutes. You still want to go to that movie tonight?"

"Yeah. If I get some work done. Do you see her a lot?"

"On and off. What's your paper on?"

"Oh, you know. The Third World thing. How come you're still seeing her?"

"Because I still want to. When's your paper due?"

"I got an extension."

"*Claire*. Are you sure you want to go a movie?"

"Yeah, I do. Because I know then I'll be able to get a lot of work done."

"Are you sure?"

"Yeah. I know I should really see it. It's the one about the World War II guy, right?"

"Right."

"And it's at the Carlton at seven?"

"Yeah, but you have to get the tickets early because it's Tuesday and it'll be sold out. So get the tickets and meet me out front at quarter to seven."

"Kay, just a sec. I have to check the pasta."

Kay waited. She looked out again. Across the street, in front of the Church of the Redeemer, two private-school boys in grey flannels were waiting at the lights. Kay tapped the edge of the second quarter against the glass.

"Okay." It was Claire's voice again. "I'm back. God, that was a big sigh, Kay. Are you still obsessing about that thing in the *Globe*?"

"No, and I don't want to talk about it."

"Okay. I haven't even seen it yet, you know. I haven't even read it. Have you talked to Mom yet?"

"No, why? Did she call you? What did she say?"

"She said it was typical."

"Typical? Typical of what?"

"You know, typical Toronto. You know how Mom is about Toronto and the media."

"Did you talk to Dad?"

"He wasn't home. Anyway, Mom probably left a message on your machine."

Kay flinched at this news and put the quarter back in her pocket. "Okay, listen, Claire, please don't be late because the movie'll get sold out."

"Okay." There was a pause. "Kay?"

"What?"

"I'm late."

"What?"

"I'm late."

Kay closed her eyes. "How late?"

"Two weeks."

"Oh, Jesus, Claire."

"I know. I gotta go now, bye. The pasta's boiling again. See you at seven." There was a click and then the sound of the dial tone. Kay held the receiver to her cheek a moment more, then slowly replaced it in its plastic cradle. Bringing her right hand to her face, she warmed the tip of her nose with her fingertips. She grabbed a mass of things from her coat pocket—an unused Kleenex caught in a paper clip, a Royal Bank bank-machine receipt (Balance: $3,517.47) with "Peggy (310) 557-6768" written on it, an unravelling tube of Clorets mints, lipstick, and some coins. She counted two dollars and five cents in change. She read the balance and the number on the bank-machine receipt. Detaching the Kleenex from the paper clip, she wiped her nose. She stared briefly at the newspaper, folded it twice and tucked it into the pages of the magazine. Then she picked up the rest of her things, stuffed the rolled-up magazine into her side pocket and left the phone booth. It was twenty after five.

Kay looked both ways on Bloor Street and turned up the collar of her coat, pulling it closer to her neck. She jumped over a mound of snow at the curb, waited for a sleek aerodynamic van to speed past her and made a bee-line for Culture's Fresh Food Restaurant. She waited in the buffet line, pretending to read the whiteboard menus, and then asked for a cranberry muffin and a large coffee to go. She paid ($1.90) and went back outside. Walking back east to 170 Bloor Street West, the building beside the Park Plaza Hotel, she stopped to look at two A-Towing truck drivers. One of them leaned against an expired parking meter while the other checked the safety chain on the front bumper of a raised-up, beige Chevette. Kay waited for one of them to see her frowning before she pulled open the door. She buzzed Suite 404 and stared at the small rectangular speaker. After a moment, a crackly but distinct voice asked who it was.

"It's Kay."

The door buzzed and Kay went in, stamping the snow off her boots. As she pressed the up-arrow button, she appraised her reflection in the mirrored brass of the elevator doors. She was pushing her bangs to one side when the elevator arrived. The doors opened, and Kay, thinking the elevator was unoccupied, took a step and nearly collided with an unshaven man in a soiled, worn-out fireman's jacket.

"Sorry," Kay said. The man stopped and glared at her. "Sorry," Kay said again. "I didn't see you." He didn't move. Kay stepped around him and into the elevator. She pressed 4 but the elevator doors remained open. Kay pressed the close-door button and looked at the indicator lights. She started to count to ten in her head and when she reached eight the doors finally closed.

"Fuck," Kay said aloud, when the elevator began rising. "What is everyone's problem?"

She crossed the hallway and opened the door marked Dr. J. Kovacs. Inside was a small waiting-room with two pine chairs, a glass table covered with magazines, a sturdy wooden coat rack and an oak door, which was shut. Transferring her belongings to her pants pockets, Kay hung up her coat. She unrolled the *Toronto Life* magazine and smoothed the wrinkled cover with the palm of her hand. Then she sat in the chair nearest the oak door and removed the crescent-shaped piece from the plastic coffee lid. She slid this into her pocket. Putting the coffee and the magazine on the glass table, she leaned to one side. She was just bringing the unravelling tube of Clorets out of her pants pocket when the oak door opened (revealing a second oak door behind it), and in walked Dr. Judith Kovacs, a short, smiling woman whose fuzzy black hair was pulled back in a large, puffy roll.

She turned to smile softly at Kay. "Kay, come in, come in." She spoke with a pronounced Polish accent.

Kay, smiling in reflex, grabbed her coffee, and stood up. Dr. Kovacs stood aside as Kay passed through the two doorways. Kay crossed the carpet and settled herself on a leather sofa. She watched the doctor close the two doors and pull a pad of white paper out of a file drawer. Then Dr. Kovacs sat down in a black leather armchair beside her desk, adjusting a padded back-support while Kay glanced quickly around the room, letting her eyes rest for a moment on the Oriental rug, the books in the bookshelves, the seascape above the desk, the window ...

"So." Dr. Kovacs reached across her desk for a clipboard and pen. "I have not seen you in a long time."

Kay took a drink of her coffee. "It's only been a month," she said.

"I know, but it seems longer. How are you?"

"Oh, you know, fine. Discounting a few catastrophes, I'm fine." Kay put the mints beside her on the sofa. "I saw Jordan on the street the other day, and he treated me like a complete stranger."

Dr. Kovacs nodded her head.

"Claire's screwing up at school and might be pregnant. Will won't stop giving me lectures. The *Globe and Mail* slammed "Agenda," and we're probably going to get cancelled. And of course it's February, so add a foot of slush to that, and you've got my month."

"But how are you?"

"I don't know. I'm fine. I'm fine for an uptight white girl." Kay hesitated. She was looking at the design in the rug. There were red gryphons and phoenixes in opposite corners, a maze-like pattern of swirling flowers in the middle, and some squat-looking amphoras along its border. She looked up. "I feel like one of those glass things. Just as the snow settles down, somebody comes along and shakes it up again. I feel like there's all this *stuff* around me that I have to keep track of. It's so distracting. I finally had to write it all down."

"You wrote it down?"

Kay took another sip of coffee. There was a small silence. "Do you have it?"

"No. It was just a list. " Kay located a loose thread in the inseam of her pants. She took one hand off her coffee, caught the thread and twirled it back and forth between her index finger and thumb. "I don't know. I was thinking it's hard to explain stuff like that and not have people distort what you mean. Like with Jordan, when we were going out ... You know, people set up all these weird geometries for each other. I mean, say you meet someone and you think they're going to think of you in a certain way, so you react to that. Like you pretend you're the person they think you are, or—or then you realize, that's not how they really think of you, you know? You react to all these imagined alliances and ... I mean they're over there, and you think they're over here, and there's like all these entanglements between the two. I don't know. I was just thinking about Claire and Will and that they both have this idea of what I should be and what I should do and how that stuff can bug you sometimes."

Kay drew a breath. She looked up into Dr. Kovacs's impassive face. Kay caught the black thread again, gripped it tightly at its base and with a quick tug snapped it off. She looked up and frowned at the seascape. Kay looked at it as if there were something about it she didn't like. "That painting behind you's still a bit crooked."

Dr. Kovacs, silent, had not looked away from Kay. "Tell me about your list."

Kay crossed her arms. "It was nothing important, really. Just dumb, stupid stuff. About work."

"When did you write it?"

"After work. I'm not supposed to know this woman I work with is getting fired. Which is fine, really, because three or four times a day she comes over to my desk and complains about stupid this and stupid that. Probably we'll all get fired ... The *Globe* piece was so depressing."

"The *Globe*?"

Kay nodded. "Yeah, they ran a column about the show. They said we're biased and under-researched. Which are pretty serious criticisms, considering that we're supposed to be a media watchdog show. But it's just a dinky little half-hour. And bias is only a problem if you hide it. I know even the idea of the CBC having a watchdog show is hard to take seriously, because it *is* the Canadian media to a certain extent. But imagine the *Globe* attacking the CBC for having a bias—it's like your parents fighting. It's inevitable. And boring. TV thinks print is dead. And then of course print comes down on television because print thinks all television is fluff. Do you know how ridiculous this would seem to someone in New Brunswick...?" Kay's voice trailed off. She looked at where the loose thread had been. Then she shook her head. "I'm getting to the point again where I hate Toronto. I mean, you can't go anywhere without sticking your nose in other people's business. The place is full of it."

"Yet you left Montreal."

"I know. I've been back nine months and already I feel like I've been here too long. Everybody's so *nervous*. And I'm at the point where I hate hearing about this person's new show or that person's opening or that I have to see someone else's performance piece. That's why I stopped reading NOW magazine. It's so full of people doing things."

"Are you jealous?"

"Of the NOW people? No. I'm not jealous. I'm not jealous, just—" Kay turned to the window. She finished her coffee and made herself take a deep breath. "No," she said. "It's good to be in a city where things are happening ... It's like when you're young you think you're going to just grow into this life you've imagined. But then it never seems to start. That's the thing with Claire. She's young enough not to worry about the future. I mean she's got to realize that it's now. That her life is now. That this is it. It's like that thing when someone asks you where you'll be in three years. I just add three years to my age and worry that I won't have achieved anything yet."

Kay scratched under her chin. Her muffin sat in the paper bag at her feet.

Dr. Kovacs was moving her pen in very quick counter-clockwise circles across her clean pad of paper. She looked at Kay. "But you *are* doing things, Kay."

"Yeah, I know. And I mean I'm not about to quit my job over a lousy article in the *Globe*. I need the job. But what I really want to do is finish the script so I won't have to work for anymore assholes. And if I have to sit through another story meeting where everyone agrees with one another, I'll go crazy."

Kay turned to look out the window again but it was dark now. She threw her head back on the sofa. "Am I your last appointment?" she asked, looking at the ceiling.

"Why?"

Kay brought her head down and looked Dr. Kovacs in the eye. "You want to go home early?"

"That's very clever," said Dr. Kovacs, smiling. "But, no."

Kay made a little mock-scream and slumped down in her seat, deflated. In the bookcase beneath the window, she saw a *Comprehensive Textbook of Psychology*, an *Abnormal Psychology*, a *Family Psychiatry*, two thick blue *Handbook of Clinical Behaviours*, a whole shelf of brown *Modern Symptoms of Psychology*, and some smaller volumes with blurry gold titles.

Kay watched as Dr. Kovacs finished writing. "Claire's just all over the place," she remarked, picking up the Clorets and popping one into her mouth. "Right now she's on this kick where she wants to go to art college. But it's not going to work because she's creating these huge scenarios with her room-mates and her landlord and her—the people she sleeps with—so she'll have an excuse for fucking up in her courses. She always gets halfway through something then thinks she can start something else that'll be easier. And how she could get pregnant ... It's just so irresponsible."

Dr. Kovacs dropped her head slightly and began absent-ly flicking one eyelash over and over again.

"She'll have an abortion, of course," Kay continued. "She'll have to. It's taking her five years to get a B.A. What would she do with a baby?"

Shifting in her chair, Dr. Kovacs picked up her pen again.

"I'm not even sure she's pregnant." Kay paused, as if she were about to abandon the idea, then went on. "But let's face it, Claire lies all the time. She's always lied. So it wouldn't surprise me. She's never lied about anything important, just stupid things, like she'll say she didn't borrow my coat or it wasn't her who ate the ham in the fridge. Or that she quit smoking. She went a whole year once not smoking around me because she thought I thought she'd quit. It was so silly. She's like that with Mom and Dad, too. As far as they knew, she never left school. She didn't tell them when she went to Israel. She just left. And when they found out, she told them it was for her philosophy and religions course. But she wouldn't lie about this. I don't think she'd lie about this. When we lived together it was a nightmare. But I don't know that she would lie about being pregnant."

"She can arrange to have an abortion, can't she?"

"Yes, of course she can, but it just seems so damned unnecessary. I mean, Claire thinks everything always works out and that nothing ever affects her. Which drives me crazy. It's so *careless*. I mean I'm not going to lay some heavy trip on her about it, but she has to accept responsibility sometime. It was the same thing with Jordan. Well, it wasn't exactly the same thing. Jordan never got pregnant." Kay looked at Dr. Kovacs. "But he always relied on other people to work out his problems."

"How did that make you feel?"

"About being one of those people?" Kay said. "I don't know. Feeling responsible for other people is dumb, isn't it?"

"Is it?"

Kay sighed. "I suppose I wouldn't want Claire to feel responsible for me." She looked again at the darkened window. "Fuck. I'll probably have to get a new job now, though. Great. Claire'll be pregnant, and I'll be unemployed. We could've stayed in Moncton to do that."

Dr. Kovacs pressed herself back into her chair. Then she folded her hands on her lap.

"I hate to think about her going through all of that crap," Kay said. "Your body takes a long time to adjust. I mean, at least I was a little older and Jordan went with me, and Patrick is not what I would call a compassionate guy. I just hate the thought of her walking into that clinic and filling out all those forms, sitting around in the waiting room, trying to act comfortable. I mean that will really screw her up at school. And the ceiling-stuff. That kind of thing really gets to Claire."

"What is the ceiling-stuff?"

"The ceiling at the clinic where I had my abortion. Remember?" Kay crunched the half-sucked mint in her back teeth. "The dogs."

Dr. Kovacs shook her head and put her pen down.

"I think I told you. Well, after you fill everything out and get your tax receipt, you go upstairs to this other waiting room. Then a nurse makes you take a sedative, and she sends you upstairs again where another nurse—though they look more like waitresses than nurses—checks your blood and gives you a shot. You wait in another room until another nurse comes out and calls your name. Meanwhile all these, well, not all these but about three other women are lying in La-Z-Boys looking tired and sick. But everybody is really, really nice and casual. Like it's no big deal. Then the nurse gets you to sit in between the stirrups and some doctor appears and other nurses flit around in the background. And the nurse, mine's name was Cathy, she sits there and shows you the gas mask and says to breathe in when it hurts."

Kay sat up straighter, leaning away from the sofa and towards Dr. Kovacs. She was speaking a little faster now. "So I'm lying there, trying to adjust this mask, and Cathy takes my hand. It wasn't unnatural or awkward, just a simple little gesture. I'm lying there trying not to feel nervous while the doctor's opening me up, so of course I look at the ceiling. And what's taped to the ceiling but all of these snapshots of dogs. I couldn't believe it. Dogs. Tons of them. It's like every person who works there has a dog and they all put their pictures up to give us something to chat about. I'm lying with my feet in stirrups, my socks bunched up around my ankles, a stranger holding my hand and some man digging around my uterus, looking for whatever the hell the last man left in there, and you can't help but try to match the dog to the doctor. 'Well, he's got the Lab, and I bet she's got the Pekinese ...' And you're laughing, probably a little high on the gas when Cathy says, 'It's going to hurt for a minute here' and then it does."

Kay sat back on the sofa and widened her eyes, unfocussing them. "Then it was over. I just lay there for a second, looking at those stupid pictures, feeling ashamed because I knew Cathy had little imprints of my fingernails in her hand." She cleared her throat. "And I thought my job was stressful. They should get medals, those women. They must never be able to get away from their work."

Kay's gaze passed over the desk and stopped on the metal part of Dr. Kovacs's clipboard. "Anyway, for some reason, when

Claire told me, the first thing I thought of was those dogs."

Kay looked up. Dr. Kovacs was examining her pen. "Haven't I told you that story before?"

"No."

"I thought I had. Funny how I thought of Claire, though."

Dr. Kovacs nodded and shifted in her chair.

"And now Claire wants to go to *art* college in Nova Scotia. First it was oceanography, then it was English, and now it's art history. She says she has to be by the ocean now." Kay shrugged. She looked at the painting again. "That's Lake Ontario, isn't it?" she said abruptly.

Dr. Kovacs nodded.

"God, I didn't know where it was. I kept thinking it was Gdansk or somewhere." Kay laughed, then, immediately, she frowned. She swallowed a remaining piece of mint. "And Will," she said. "Will's been phoning me about fifty times a day because his new boyfriend's driving him crazy." Kay fingered some hair out of her eye. In the corner, on the filing cabinet, stood a small brass clock. It was six-fifteen.

"Let's see," Dr. Kovacs said, reaching across the desk, past a glass paperweight of frozen bubbles, past postcards and papers, for a leather date-book. "Do I have any more appointments for you?"

"Yeah. Just one."

"Do you want more for next month?"

"Nah, I'm okay for now."

Dr. Kovacs wrote in her book. Kay put the empty coffee cup in the paper bag, picked up the bag, and stood. Dr. Kovacs closed her book.

"Good. Good. You have a good week, Kay."

"Thanks, Judith. You, too."

Kay walked through the double doors into the waiting room. She was pulling her scarf off the coat rack when the outside door opened. A middle-aged couple bustled in. Pretending that she was having a little trouble threading her arm into her sleeve, Kay turned her head for a moment, and instead of meeting the couples's eyes, she looked slightly over their heads. After buttoning her coat, she gave them a brief smile and walked out.

As Kay Pritchard was waiting for her elevator, Dickie Candelaria was hanging up his and his wife's winter coats on the coat rack. Helen Candelaria was already sitting in one of the pine chairs, folding her faded fox fur on her lap. She brushed some remnants of snow off her thick wool skirt. Dickie, after patting down the thinning hair on the top of his head, walked stiffly across the room to the other chair. He sat down and picked up a magazine. Someone had been scribbling on it. Crossing his right leg over his left and narrowing his eyes, he brought the magazine closer to his face and read:

> results, the prospects of discovery, being discovered, Virgin, afraid of flying, diving, driving, dogs, sex, food, death, illness, lesbians, fags, blacks, drugs, drug dealers, cigarettes, addiction, friends, lovers, men, others, fathers, over-aggressive siblings, overly-dependent siblings, parents-in-law, teachers, professors, stupidity, anger, anguish, alcohol, assholes, angels, Jordan, animals, animists, cancer, shit, piss, penises, uncircumcised penises in particular, genitals in general, generals, Jesus, Jews, God, (not the Holy Ghost), swimming, oceans, seaweed, fish, sharks, shields, armies, trojans, navies, wars, weirdness in the streets, weirdness in the sheets, people who say weird, women, brains, beauty, body odour, parachuting, sky diving, skin diving, deep sea diving, dedications, drudgery, rap music, rap artists, rapists, feminists, dykes on bikes, bizarro cartoons, left-wing loonies, right-wing nightmares, capitalists, socialists, Communists, Marxists, Leninists, existentialists, hedonists, linguists, deconstructionists, deconstructivists, post-structuralists, minimalists, wine lovers, gourmands, yuppies, WASPs, convicts, pederasts, pedophiles, priests, palaces, Prince, princes, princess, paranormal

Claire

WHAT IS IT WITH this place? And what is it about a city that makes people feel they have to know everything? And I thought all that stuff about Toronto the Good was Victorian bunkum left over from Orangemen Parades and Black Watch regiments, but I mean, God, people get so uptight about their lives here. It's ridiculous. What exactly are they trying to perfect?

When I first moved to Toronto about a year and a half ago, I lived with Kay on Euclid Avenue, and because I had absolutely zero money, Kay got me a job as a production assistant on this cheesy spy movie starring Christopher Plummer. Except he wasn't really the star, in fact he only did two days' work. *But he got paid forty thousand dollars.* I mean, that's more than I've made in five years. And the thing was, they weren't even hard days. All he had to do was sit around and have a couple drinks with the junior spies. Forty thousand dollars because he was Captain Von Trapp in *The Sound of Music.* He was okay in that, he was good, and I still watch it at Christmas when it's on TV, but isn't it just a little ridiculous that he can go on making twenty thousand dollars a day because he lip-synched "Edelweiss"?

Being around Christopher Plummer is weird, though, because you don't know if you should make jokes and be yourself or not. I sat at the same lunch table as he did, and he's very polite, but when you first spend time around celebrities, you really don't know what to expect. And you want to pretend that you've *done* something brilliant too, like travelled around the world or composed a concerto. And you prepare yourself for all these really probable situations like, "What if Christopher Plummer gets a crush on me? What do I do if he asks me out?" Right. When really at two a.m. at the wrap party, it's one of the gaffer guys who ends up patting your hand for an hour, telling you you have the most beautiful skin of anyone in Canada. But that guy, he was a nice gaffer guy and coming home that night I thought that I'd been kind of snobby to him when I didn't need to be, and that was the first time when I thought, Fuck, maybe I'm becoming a Toronto person.

I still feel that way, like even when I'm out with Patrick or Liz I'm kind of astounded at the things I hear myself say. It's strange because sometimes I feel really comfortable talking and spending time with them, and other times I don't, and I think even now none of us has really established any way of getting along. Well, maybe Patrick and Liz have.

Liz and I lived together my last year at McGill. Actually, she'd sort of been in the background of my life for a long time. I met her when I was visiting my cousin in Halifax when I was ten. And again at a gymnastic meet in PEI, and then in first-year McGill her room-mate, Gail, was in two of my classes. I had a feeling she was going to turn up again so I wasn't surprised when one day at the end of second year I ran into Liz on St. Catherine. She told me she and Gail needed another person for a flat they'd found on Prince Arthur. It was an enormous place with high ceilings and tall windows and long hallways, so I said yes. I loved it. In fact, it's still my all-time favourite apartment.

Liz and Gail knew each other from Halifax, and since I grew up in Moncton and was a fellow Maritimer, we thought it would be a convivial match. Which it was, pretty much. Although I kind of hate thinking about those years in Montreal because I feel like I totally wasted most of my time there. I can't really remember, for example, what I did that year on Prince Arthur. I mean, I returned to that apartment practically every day for two hundred days and all I can remember is about twelve cold dark winter nights staying up late with Gail and Liz, eating popcorn, going out for bagels or arguing about whatever: ourselves, our friends, food, men, sex.

When I left McGill that March and decided to go to the Middle East, Liz was one of the few people I kept in touch with. I don't know why, exactly, because she certainly wasn't my closest friend, but when she gave up the apartment to do her M.A. in political theory at U of T, she sent my stuff to Ottawa. I was impressed when I heard about the M.A. In fact, whenever I heard of someone making a firm decision like that, I always felt a little crazy. But all through her M.A. Liz kept firing off postcards and letters to me, telling me who was happening to whom, inviting me to visit and arranging for me to stay with her sister in London.

And Liz was one of the few people who didn't say I was crazy for going. Because I know people all sort of laughed at me for going to Israel. I wasn't really very organized when I left, and I did end up kind of spaced out at a yoga camp in Mexico, but it wasn't a complete waste of time. Ostensibly, the reason for the trip was to be with Jacob, a guy I was in love with, but it didn't really work out. Sometimes, when you're desperately attracted to somebody you just try to be what he wants you to be. And you know it's stupid but you still poke around to see what part of you he likes. You can be anorexic, or grow your hair, or get a degree, or see a lot of art films—or go to Israel and work on a Moshav. Basically you just want him to notice you. But when I got to Israel and realized I was never going to meet his parents, and when he wanted me to stay in a hotel in Haifa instead of his home, I just thought, Fuck, this is stupid. So I left and went back to London and worked in this depressing pub before finding a cheap flight to Puerto Vallarta.

When I finally got out of Mexico and came waltzing matilda back to Ottawa, I kind of collapsed and there was like this blah period of about eight months when I had or didn't have post-viral syndrome or Epstein-Barr virus or Chronic Fatigue syndrome or whatever you want to call it. In any case, I lost about twenty pounds and stopped having my period for six nerve-wracking months and had to be hospitalized with a fever of a hundred and four. But when I finally felt healthy again and I'd rid myself of doctors, I decided to visit Liz in Toronto, seeing how I hadn't been there since Kay was at York. I took the train down, and after I stowed my stuff at Liz and Tasha's apartment on Palmerston (where, as it happens, I'm living now) we went out for dinner at an Indian restaurant. This was like two years ago.

Now, the Toronto Liz was like a totally different person. I was amazed at the transformation. She'd created this "Liz person". She was pretty convincing, too, and I could tell a lot of people believed her. They wanted to believe her, because if it was Liz, she'd be kind of perfect. Not like *Little Women* perfect, but kind of the absolute antithesis, which is another kind of perfect. But it wasn't her. I mean, it wasn't the real Liz. It wasn't the Liz I knew—and in a way I could tell she was glad I knew it She wore her hair long and dark and unstyled. Eye-liner and lipstick only, and this from a girl who once had a subscription to Bonne Bell cosmetics. And instead of the L. L. Bean stuff she used to wear at McGill, she had on a paisley T-shirt and a black leather jacket borrowed from someone named Tyborg (Tee-bohr). Now that her braces were gone, the corners of her mouth kind of moved down when she spoke, like she was pushing her jaw a bit forward as a kind of joke. And she talked with a weird irony that was sort of scornful and enthusiastic at the same time. It was a real McGill accent, which was funny, because when we were there, she didn't have it. At least, I don't think so. But now that she was in Toronto she had it, and for some reason it made me think even more that I was stupid not to have finished my degree, that I was stupid to have gone to Israel, and that if I wanted to do anything in my life I'd better be better educated—a thought I still have about two hundred times a day.

After dinner, Liz started telling me about this guy whose leather jacket she was wearing. He was from Vancouver, he was in the program for Social and Political Thought at York, and his name was Tyborg Todowski. Tyborg Todowski. What a great name. I don't know why, exactly, but from the way Liz was talking, I pictured a tall dark-haired man in a blue suit standing in front of the Brandenberg Gate. Because obviously your ideas of wonderful men are hard to separate from the men you've seen in magazines and in films. So it's kind of anticlimactic when you meet him because Tyborg's losing his hair—in fact the skin on his head is so shiny you think he's going to go bald any minute, right in front of you—but he's actually one of the most generous people I've met here.

Liz said that Tyborg wasn't entirely sure he wanted to be an academic. He was also trying to get a band together. "He's got a piano," she said, "and all these computers and keyboards and samplers in the apartment. He's been working on a set of compositions for the last seven years ..." Her voice kind of trailed off, then she looked at me. "But besides, it's the best sex of my life."

Now Liz was pretty inhibited in Montreal, really kind of a sneaky-weird repressed person, especially about sex. I remember there was one night when Gail and I were talking about which of our male friends we'd sleep with, just call up and sleep with, nothing more. We started constructing a list of qualifications for the ideal no-attachment-night-of-sex man, and I remember the only thing Liz came up with was that he should be the kind of man who noticed neck-lengths, not breast size, and she thought of him as having a rather casual long-standing relationship with an intelligent mystery woman who was, as she said, "too weird to put out".

Anyway, at the time I was talking to Liz in the restaurant I was kind of in a celibate phase. I'd been sexless for about a year, since a ridiculous night in Mexico, so I was almost jealous at the mere mention of a bladder infection, let alone the greatest sex of someone's life. So of course I had to ask her. "How do you mean, the best sex?"

Liz picked up some seeds from a fake silver clamshell on the table. "Well," she said, cracking the seeds between her teeth, "I'm having these really—violent *orgasms* lately."

I couldn't even remember Liz saying the word before.

"That's great," I said.

"Yeah, I don't know. It's peculiar, though. I don't know what's happening and I can't predict—I can't foresee what they're going to be like. You know, when you go all blurry and have to grab onto something. Tyborg says I practically throw him out of bed."

"So it's only been with Tyborg?"

"Oh," Liz said, kind of pushing her hair back. "Oh yeah. It's just curious because it's never happened before." Anyway, she went on like that. You could tell she wanted to talk about it. To tell you the truth, I think it was all kind of new to her. It was still kind of depressing, though.

Sex is so crazy. Until about two weeks ago, I could count all the people I've slept with on two hands. Then I sort of had to start using toes. But I still remember how obscure and even scary sex seemed, especially growing up in Moncton. Sex started for me when I was fifteen, back when I felt incredibly lucky just to be going out and holding hands with someone—though at the time I was also terrified I was the only girl in history with a hair on her nipple. When I was fifteen, I went steady with Iain White who was sixteen, and after our second date he walked me to our back door and kissed me in the fog for about twenty minutes. A few months later, Kevin LeBlanc, my second boyfriend, kissed my neck and I just about melted. But what really made me crazy when I was fifteen was the thought of someone going down on me—oh my God, I could hardly stand it. I kept imagining how it must feel and when it finally did happen, to have that feeling you've had before but that always went away, to have it keep going and going until the end of the world as I knew it, well, I didn't want it to stop. Ever. It was The Best Thing That Had Ever Happened To Me In My Life. None of the first guys would do it, of course, they didn't even know you could.

The first guys I ended up sleeping with were really uptight—guys who were more afraid of sex than I was, though I didn't realize that until two years ago. It's funny when you're visiting your grandmother in Moncton three years later, and you run into those guys at the mall looking for barbecue coals with their fiancées. You look at them and think, Oh yeah, I've slept with him—I've *had* him, how weird and kind of ridiculous.

My first time was with a guy my sister Kay went to high school with, Mike McGuire, in his parents' bed when they were in Tampa. A real square student council geek, but with a great ass. He's in Med School now at Western. My God, he was nervous. We went out for six months? Something like that.

Number Two was Walker something, can't remember his last name. A fling in a closet when I visited Kay during Thanksgiving at York when I was in grade eleven. He was a theatre student, then a bassist, then a bike courier, then last I heard he was driving zodiacs for Greenpeace in Vancouver.

Number Three. Michael Esterbrooks, in the back of his

van after we'd bought condoms at the Lawton's Drugstore in Riverview Mall. A pothead drug-dealer with a little greebly moustache. We were stoned for half of grade twelve.

Number Four. Aubrey McKee. Or MacTavish. A friend of a friend during Welcome Week at McGill. One of those try-everything world-traveller guys. Don't know where he is now. We were both incredibly smashed but he maintained a hard dink after eight or nine drinks.

Number Five. Jacob Waxman, in Montreal, second year McGill, with a little stammer saying my name. Up to that time, the most accomplished man I had ever met, and I admired him way too much. I thought he was a genius. He's at Oxford now doing a Ph.D. in Aramaic, the language Jesus spoke. A beautiful silky cock, or penis if you prefer. Cocks. Dinks. Pricks. Weenies. Penises. That selfish, benign, cute, dull, plodding little thing which, for all its stupidity, manages more often than not to get its way. Jacob and I went out off and on for eighteen months. Probably mostly off. Though at the time I would have said on.

Number Six. On the way to Israel. A greasy but handsome Scottish guy when I was hiking on the moors. Had very soft nipples.

Number Seven. Doesn't really count as a new person—it was Jacob again in Israel—in a fleabag hotel in downtown Haifa because Jacob's aunt was dying at his house. Jacob told me his mother constantly called me "the shiksa," which I thought was kind of exotic, though Jacob was very insulted by it. But sleeping with him then was a mistake, I know that now. The first shouldn't-have-but-did.

Number Eight. On the rebound with an uncircumcised Australian frisbee guy I met on the beach in Mexico. The first what-am-I-doing-but-oh-okay. We were stoned and he kept losing his concentration and couldn't come. It was dumb, cliché sex too, like when you hear yourself say all the things everybody says: "I want to feel you inside me." "You feel so good." "I want you." "Tell me when you're going to come." "Oh, your hands feel so good." "Fuck me, fuck me." "I love it when you come." "Harder." "Faster." "Deeper." "Stop." "Don't stop." "Stop." But, of course, any words sound stupid when you're having sex because sex is really a language of touching and being touched, and no matter what you say, it doesn't really apply. You just *like* things, like how freshly-washed hair feels after sex, or muscles in people's legs, or shivers, and I'll tell you, the best lovers are the ones who enjoy women who enjoy sex. Of course, each relationship, each person, is unique, but I'll tell you two other things I've learned. Don't be afraid to ask for what you want. And if you're spending more time talking about sex or your relationship than having it, then it's probably over. And you have to be smart enough to realize that. That took me a long time to learn. It took me until Patrick to learn that, and Patrick Manning was Number Nine.

That night at the Indian restaurant with Liz I decided I wanted to go back to school and finish my degree because it would be a step in the right blah blah blah. I didn't want to go back to Montreal, though, because I was sick of all the anglophones bumming cigarettes from each other, arguing about the future of Quebec, and I didn't want to go to Carleton and live at home, so within six months of my conversation with Liz, I was sitting in these tutorials at U of T with all these super-smart students who'd all read ten times what I'd read and who talked very assuredly about anxieties of influence and deconstruction. Patrick was totally into deconstruction, of course. He met Derrida at a linguistics conference in Glasgow—they talked over bangers and mash one breakfast—so he was a complete convert for a while. Sometimes I space out and have these mental blocks where for some reason I get stuff totally mixed up.

Like last summer I was at a party complaining about the stupid deconstruction commercials they had on TV, and everyone started to look really uncomfortable. It wasn't until two days later that I realized I was talking about Dianetics. It's kind of a perpetually humbling experience finding out every six months what an asshole you used to be.

Toronto. Yikes. Coming from New Brunswick, even coming from Ottawa, I couldn't believe how much money there was. There's so much money here. I mean, in New Brunswick, a million dollars is a lot of money. There's probably only about eight people who have a million dollars in New Brunswick, including the Irvings and the McCains. But here there must be ten thousand people with a million dollars. Or probably more. It's kind of ridiculous, at parties meeting the children of cabinet ministers and World Bank presidents and factory owners ... or Christopher Plummer.

God, I was ready to work like two zillion per cent on that movie, but it was so schlocky and the second A.D. was such a terrible asshole that after a while I didn't care. Most of the time I just waited around anyway, pretending I had something to do, though one time I did stay up all night helping the set dressers make a parking lot look more New York-y, sticking New York license plates on cars, dragging around *USA Today* boxes and American phone booths. None of which we used, incidentally, because they didn't have enough time to get the shot before they lost the daylight. Which I knew was going to happen. And the second A.D., who had yelled at us for two days to finish it, he didn't even thank us. They don't understand simple things, those guys. Like how to say thank you. I don't know how Kay puts up with them. She always says if you're willing to do it, you can do shit work for two years and become a producer, but even as a producer, I couldn't put up with that second A.D. That guy generally behaved as if we were in a plane crash, that he was the only one who could be trusted to make decisions, and the rest of us were the ungrateful retarded orphans he had to lead to safety. With him, you could never do anything right. It was like being stuck in an eternal Mormon commercial.

Anyway, my first year at U of T was kind of absurd because I had no idea what degree I should get or what courses I should take because it was a total fucking drag transferring credits from McGill; bureaucratic U of T only gave me ten out of fourteen credits, so that's why it's taking me two years to finish. Last year I was taking a Theory of Romanticism course at Victoria College. And I had a big crush on one of the T.A.s, I didn't know his name, but he looked like William Hurt's intelligent younger brother. He wasn't Adonis or anyone, I mean he didn't have the greatest body in the world, and he had one of those thin North American bums, the kind where the leg turns into the bum without a bump, but he had a nice way about his shoulders. And he was tall and had long blond hair and round dark-rimmed glasses like Jean-Paul Sartre. I used to see him around the city: crossing the street, at the bank machine, and I met his eyes once when he was in a movie line-up at the Bloor Cinema. *Fitzcarraldo* was the movie, I think.

One day during reading week last February I went out to look for a copy of *The Faerie Queen* in the second-hand bookstores on Harbord Street. I needed it for this essay I was doing on mutability. It was a beautiful day, with the sun coming through the clouds like a God-poster and the trees silhouetted against the sky. I didn't feel like starting the essay right that minute so I kept on walking and I ended up on Palmerston and I thought I'd drop in on Liz and Tyborg.

I let myself in, still vaguely wondering what dweeby old Edmund Spenser would think of the biceps on the beautiful red-haired dyke who worked out at the athletic centre. As I came in, Liz was standing in front of the love-seat, her back to me, looking down at none other than the gorgeous T.A. guy, William Hurt's younger brother. His hair was in a pony-tail, and he wore a black turtleneck sweater and a sports jacket. He was smiling up at Liz, smiling as if he'd just heard the punch-line of a joke, then he noticed me.

"Hi, Claire," Liz said, turning around. She was wearing a cat suit, and her hair was swept up on top of her head. The T.A. stood up and introduced himself as Patrick Manning. He said his name twice. I said my name, and he raised his eyebrows a little and smiled a close-lipped polite smile, and for a split-second I worried that he'd read something I'd written for the Romanticism class, which would have been terrible because I didn't know how to write an essay last year.

Liz poured me a glass of wine and sat down on the love-seat beside Patrick. "I was just telling Patrick that Tyborg bought a thirty-thousand-dollar digital recording machine this morning," she said, looking at me.

"That's great," I said.

Liz looked to Patrick. "Not really. He borrowed most of the money, and he's thinking of quitting school."

"Well maybe he'll finish his songs and be able to sell them."

Liz rolled her eyes. "He doesn't want to hurry the songs, and besides, he said he made a pact with the music not to play it to anyone. He doesn't want to do violence to his inspiration by forcing it into something. Doesn't want to 'extort the music for personal gain,' was the way he put it."

"He made a pact?"

Liz nodded.

"So you haven't heard any of it?"

"No. No one's heard it."

"*Ay Caramba*. That's kind of incredible," I said. I think I had this vision of Liz and Tyborg in bed, Liz reading, underlining passages of interest while Tyborg, the quiet musical genius, improvised on a keyboard at the foot of the bed. "Well, is he keeping recordings of it or writing it down?"

Liz waved one of her hands. "'The music is already out there,' he says. 'It's just a matter of finding it' or letting it find him. He just sits down and lets his fingers go all over the keyboard."

"So no one knows what it sounds like except him? You haven't heard *any* of it, Liz? Like what are they about?" I looked at Patrick. He was writing something down in a little notebook with a silver pen.

"Okay," Liz sniffed, looking at both of us. "His songs are about the recovery from suffering. He says that Mozart, whom he pronounces 'Moe's art', didn't suffer enough. His music is good, but he didn't suffer enough."

"But he likes Mozart?"

"Oh yeah," said Liz. "He likes Mozart. And early Genesis."

"Well, he's either a genius or he's crazy," I said, laughing.

"He's crazy," Patrick said, smiling and putting his pen in the inside pocket of his sportsjacket. "Mozart and early Genesis. Right."

I wasn't really sure whose benefit this conversation was for—me, Patrick or Liz herself. Liz is funny because she goes through this thing where she develops conspiracy theories about her friends, where she thinks we're all thinking the wrong things about her, and so every two years she sheds her friends and completely ignores what they're doing. It's why she doesn't see Gail anymore. And I think the day I met Patrick was like the beginning of the end for Tyborg.

I found out from Liz later that Patrick is from Brampton and he was writing a Ph.D. on Rhetorics of Authority. He is two years younger than Liz and I. His basement bachelor on Major Street was wall-to-wall books—the guy had scads of books. In-the-middle-of-reading books. Books he'd been reading last night. Books he wanted to read. Books for his thesis. I'd never seen so many in such a small place. He'd put up wooden planks and steel brackets, and row upon row of Penguin paperbacks ran along the wall, around the corners, into the bedroom, and on a special shelf above his bed was a series of modern first editions with plastic covers to protect the dust-jackets.

Most of the books seemed read, though, so I was impressed. I mean I probably have the foremost collection of unread books in the city. Patrick read Nietzche, Artaud, Freud, Bœthius, Mallarmé, Heidegger, Catullus, Juvenal, Mill, Hegel, blah blah blah … I haven't read any of those guys. Except Hegel and Freud. I've read little snatches of them.

Patrick called me after that impromptu meeting at Liz's and asked me if I was interested in hearing a lecture his adviser was giving. Another time we had dinner with Tyborg and Liz, and around Easter we went to *The Story of Adèle H*. I wasn't sure, but from what Liz said, I took it that Patrick was either getting over a relationship or in the process of extricating himself from one.

One night we ran into each other coming out of a photo-copy shop on College, and we went for coffee. Patrick was in a really pumped-up mood because, after a year of trying, he had finally, with his adviser's help, gotten a paper accepted in an academic quarterly. And when Patrick gets going, he talks non-stop in whole paragraphs of heavy-duty jargon. Literary criticism—the whole history of interpretation in general—was one thing he really loved.

I asked him if he didn't go crazy with all the isms. I remember he was wearing his Jean-Paul Sartre glasses, although he said he didn't wear them much anymore because he hated people who wore them. He looked up from his apple fritter and took off his glasses. "It's true, it's true. A lot of critical theory is garbage, but you have to be intellectually pessimistic. And spiritually optimistic." But later on, coming back from the men's room, he said he'd deconstructed that statement and found it was impossible to separate the two.

Patrick has crazy likejs and dislikes. He loves films, but he hates videos. In fact he doesn't even own a television, and when I moved into his place last summer, we had a fight about whether or not I should bring mine with me. And then of course after I moved in he watched it all the time. Anyway, about a month later, I finally got around to reading that paper he published in the *Queen's Quarterly*. It was titled "Against the Romantic Dynamic: Theories of Modern Self" by P. Patrick Manning, and it was practically unreadable. Ostensibly it was about biography in the 1800s, but it was so full of psychologistic consequences and extra-linguistic realities that it took me three readings just to begin to figure out what the hell he was talking about. Kay always says Patrick is one of those people who keeps looking around when he's talking to you, as if he's expecting to see someone he knows. And that's exactly the feeling I got when I read that essay.

I got it again when I read the letter Patrick left me three weeks ago when he, well, left me. We'd been arguing about really dumb little things. We'd have these crazy long arguments that would start off being about the sound my boots made on the sidewalk but that would end up being about whether I should tug on his ear in public or Salman Rushdie should remain in hiding. Relationships can be so ludicrous. I mean, you would never register your disapproval with a friend for how they cut a tomato. But Patrick and I, we fought for half a morning about *how to cut a tomato*. And in every argument he'd put on this snarky little voice and do this thing where he'd push his hair behind his ear and stare at me like "What are you doing in my apartment?" And when I started to have that fantasy where after we break up his parents die, and I am the only person he can talk to, and he tells me he wants us to get back together, I knew things were really bad. I can't remember what it was that made him write the letter, and I still don't know what he's talking about.

Dear Claire,

I imagine you reading this, reading it at once sedate and nervous. Always so nervous, Claire, and you don't like being nervous. People draw a certain strength from nervousness. But not too much, lest they seem what? Overbearing, I guess.

I wrote that cryptic first line because as soon as I wrote your name I wanted to consider what you said to me yesterday. I know you feel I misrepresent things, but to say that my decisions were unfairly representing me, were in fact going against my own best nature (What is that, a "best nature?"), I can't begin to express how much I disagree with such a view. I resent the implication that I subdue or disavow something in my feelings for you, and I resent the cautious duplicity that goes along with the suggestion.

I know it seems I am looking to lay blame somewhere, and that's not good. And this is a cruel letter as it is, an angry letter, but it's been made so by these last few weeks. Certainly I'm angry that I've let myself become angry, but maybe anger was the only way things could be said. And things needed to be said.

I feel your pain and censure, your sense of betrayal and loss, as I write, but I can't live with your point of view in mind, Claire; that's for you to do. And in a way I felt betrayed myself, being privy to all those thoughts and fears. For beneath the stubborn hold on analysis there is fear. You're ashamed of yourself, Claire, and you're ashamed for other people. I think you know this but haven't yet found a way to get outside it and cope with it properly.

Liz said that every person you've gone out with has come out emotionally wasted, and I think I understand why. Yours is an insidious generosity, Claire, a sen-

sitivity so far beyond normalcy, that it amounts to betrayal if your lover cannot reciprocate in kind. The sensitivi-
ty, the modesty, the kindness, the constant awareness, the
feelings that ought to be felt, they attracted me at first
but I no longer feel their comfort. They seem weapons now.

You try to out-think yourself, Claire, and I can't
imprison myself within that way of thinking, a way of
thinking which had me becoming something I'm not.

I do things I am not always proud of, Claire; I
make mistakes. But I think it's better to judge wrongly
than to jump up and down with your hands tied ...

It went on, too, but that was the gist of it. I couldn't
believe it. I could not fucking believe I got this letter. And I
couldn't believe I was the person it was meant for—I mean, I
felt like I was supposed to grade it and send it back. I had nothing to do with the person that letter was meant for. And I can't
believe someone would actually *write* a letter like that. Patrick
was trying to come to terms with something, I guess, some
complex set of ideas or something, but it was pretty *stupid* and
pretty ill-advised to put it into writing and actually send it to
someone. I'm going to keep that letter, though, and I'm going
to send it to him when he's forty. To remind him what an asshole he was. And if I see him, I'm going to tug on his ear.

But God, poor Salman Rushdie. I still think about him.
One of the first times I went to Patrick's apartment he showed
me a signed first edition of *The Satanic Verses* which he got at the
International Authors Festival. How weird and ridiculous it is
that one day Patrick's getting him to sign a book and the next
day the book's condemned and he's sentenced to death. I mean,
sometimes I look at my own life (Claire Anne Pritchard
1967–1992+) and I wonder what the hell it has to do with anything. Like with the Soviet Union and Bosnia and people losing
their jobs, how does that figure with Tuesday's outlook is sunny

and warm and the fact that I really have to do a laundry and that two of my best friends will be getting married this summer and that if I die before I wake someone will come here, take me away, take off my clothes, put me in a nice dress, stuff my cheeks full of cotton balls, then put me in a box and show me to people I knew when I was still alive and wearing two-day-old panties. You can't maintain stuff like that in words. It's like before I go to sleep at night—Oh my God. Allan Boutilier. I slept with Allan Boutilier just before we left Moncton. I completely forgot about him. So I guess that makes Patrick number ten.

Anyway, that night before I went home for Christmas, this was like the last Friday before Christmas last year, I knew this weird factor was starting to creep in between Patrick and me. I came home from Christmas shopping and caught him wanking in front of "Star Trek: The Next Generation." Patrick is a chronic, inveterate masturbater, and he has a huge crush on Deanna Troi, the Betazoid counsellor, but he won't admit it—which makes me sick—and we proceeded to have this insanely long argument that started off being about wiping your boots when you come in the front door but which veered into how we spent too much time together and how we were distracting each other from getting our work done.

About an hour later, Liz called to ask what we were doing and went into a long tirade about Tyborg. Liz and Tyborg had suspended their relationship in November on the grounds that they should be free to see other people for a while. So Tyborg had moved out of the apartment. Liz told me on the phone that she hadn't been happy for a while, though. "It was all form and no content," she said. "I mean, I'm with this person who's supposed to be my lover and everything, but something's wrong, you know. Something's not there. So why bother discussing it?

But Tyborg won't give up, you know, he keeps calling me, and tonight he wants to take me out to dinner. But Claire, you know he just wants to suck me into a relationship talk, which I do not have time for. What are you guys doing?"

Now before the argument, Patrick and I were going to go to this giant party. Kay had called and told us that her friend Will was back in town, and he'd invited us all to a giant groover party. Personally, I wasn't crazy about seeing Liz, because I was going to Ottawa the next day for Christmas, but I was in one of those moods where I'm too scared not to be friendly so I asked Patrick if he wanted to do something with Liz. I thought he would say no because after the argument he'd said he wanted to stay in and finish a chapter of his thesis, but now it was like he wanted to go out and said sure, tell Liz we'll pick her up in a taxi at ten. So after a minute or two I felt okay about doing that and thought, Okay, we'll get dressed up and go downtown to the party and see Kay and everyone and it'll be fun. So I'm thinking what should I wear when, not really paying attention to what I'm doing, I say, "Tyborg's still calling Liz."

Patrick looks up from his computer, then kind of looks away, like he's trying to remember something. "Have you seen my pen?"

"Which pen?"

"My pen, my silver pen?"

"Oh God, Patrick," I say, "I don't keep track of your pens." So I know we're going to argue, and I feel my neck getting blotchy and red. He shakes his head and types something into the computer. Then he looks at his bookshelves. "T-Bone should grow up."

"Why?"

"It's pathetic. He can't stand to think that Liz can have a life without him."

I really like Tyborg, to tell you the truth, and in a crazy way I admire his dedication to his music. I've never come out and said it, but I think Tyborg could be a John Cage musical genius. And Patrick knew it.

"The recovery from suffering?" he says. "Jesus Christ, Claire, it's pathetic. All that suffering crap. All that self-important, self-pitying crap. It's Nineteenth-Century Romantic bullshit. *The ordeal of the self*. The feminists hate that. The smart ones hate it. And seven years? Seven years and no one's heard what he's written? Doesn't that strike you as just a tad peculiar? A little bit excessive? It's probably the best thing about it—that no one's heard it. The mystery's the only good thing. But no one will hear it, of course. Because T-Bone never finishes anything."

I said I thought Tyborg was really smart.

"Oh, he's smart," Patrick said. "But T-Bone's not that smart. And he doesn't have access to his intelligence. That's why he's so enamoured of the suffering crap."

That's when I shut up.

So Patrick and I say like two words to each other on the taxi ride down to the party. And the dumb irony is that he looks great. He's wearing his trench coat, and he's washed his hair and is wearing it loose. It looks beautiful. And there I am in the taxi, watching Patrick watch the meter, smelling the pungent B.O. of the taxi driver and realizing that we're probably going to keep getting sucked into squabbly moods all night. So as soon as we get to the party—which is wonderful by the way—I buy a bunch of drinks.

Patrick and Liz get in this deep discussion, smiling and nodding seriously at each other, no doubt deconstructing the lives of those people foolish enough not to be in grad school. I consider joining them, but then I realize I probably won't have access to their conversation. I know they aren't going to have the best time, partly because they don't know many people, but mostly because they don't know how to have fun somewhere they've never been before.

So I talk to Kay and Will and Will's new boyfriend for a while. Jordan's there, too, with a friend of his, this guy Henley, who's in a band with a name I can never remember. I've met him before with Jordan, but never let myself be attracted to him. Tonight he's kind of looking at me in this disbelieving, obvious way, sort of deferring all the conversation back to me.

There are times in my life when I look like shit, a lot of times, but there are also times when for whatever reasons all my planets and vertebrae and overall kinetic energies are in line, and I feel like I can't make a wrong move, and that night was one of them. And I notice Henley is a slim-hipped young thing who's flirting his pants off in a real silly-flirty way, like schoolboy stuff, even though you can tell he's kind of shy with a little bit of a stutter. But my guilt levels are way up for enjoying being with him, and then I think, why am I worrying? What is wrong with what I'm doing?

So I go dance like a go-go queen maniac for a while and have another drink and after we've been there about an hour, Patrick comes over and tells me that he and Liz are going to get cigarettes. The last time I see them, Patrick's listening intently to something Liz is recounting, smiling his, No-I'm-really-interested-in-that smile when he wants to seem interested but really his thoughts are probably somewhere else, and I just think, Oh please fuck off you two. And later as I'm standing there watching people dance and thinking again about how great it would be to have arm muscles, I realize I'm going to do something for myself for once, and holding on to this little minor revelation or epiphany or whatever you want to call it, I go and find that Henley guy, that cute, sweet, goofy young guy who just wants to go home with me, and, at one in the morning, when and Liz and Patrick are nowhere to be found, and I don't really want to go home and see if Patrick has or hasn't returned, I go home with Henley, take off his clothes and fuck his brains out.

Kay and Claire

IT WAS ALMOST SEVEN when Kay's taxi arrived at the Carlton cinema. She watched the driver push the yellow stop-button before she took out her wallet and gave him seven dollars. Claire was standing off to one side of the cinema doors, squinting at the approaching movie-goers and clearing some tangled hair from her eyes with a flick of her head. She didn't notice Kay till she was halfway across the street. "I couldn't get the tickets," said Claire, meeting Kay at the curb. A curl of hair slipped back across her face.

"What?"

"I got here about twenty minutes ago, but I didn't have any money. They froze my bank card."

"Why'd they do that?"

"Oh," said Claire, "I wrote these cheques that didn't really work out."

Kay looked at Claire a moment as if this were something she should have expected, then she scrutinized the line-up through the glass doors. Two people inside were waving their hands. For a moment Kay thought one of them, the man, was waving at her. She watched the fluid, supple movements of his hands for a few seconds before realizing he was deaf.

"Anyway, it's sold out," Claire said. Kay turned back to her. Beneath an unzipped black leather jacket, Claire had on a frayed, buttoned-up jean jacket with a long string of beads doubled around her neck. She wore a floral-print skirt, black leggings and red cowboy boots. "Whose jacket?" Kay asked.

"Liz's. Listen, Kay. I'm really sorry about the tickets. It's one of the movies I know I really should see. It's just that I thought my bank card would work."

Kay looked again at the line-up. Then she looked up at the marquee to see what other movies were playing. None of them appealed to her. "Oh well," she said, putting her arm around her sister. "Let's go for a walk. I'm starving. Let's make dinner."

"Are you sure?" Claire asked, reaching down to tug at the sock inside her boot. "God, I'll probably never be allowed to have a credit card."

The two women started walking west along the sidewalk.

"Who needs seats?" a man in a dirty ski-doo jacket shouted. "Who needs tickets?" His gaze passed over Kay, paused on Claire, then moved on. "Who needs hockey tickets?" In the entranceway to the Ontario Hydro building, a woman stood on a plastic milk crate, a grimy sleeping bag draped around her like a shawl. Her matted grey hair fell across her shoulders in long, congealed locks. Pointing to the people getting off the College streetcar, the woman extended her right hand and moved her fingers repeatedly, as if conferring benediction. Kay strained to hear what she was saying.

"I thought you were boycotting the Carlton, anyway," Claire said. "All the noises in the theatre, all the breathers and talkers and popcorn munchers and foot-shufflers ... you hate that stuff. We always have to move."

Kay pulled back the sleeve of her sweater and looked at her watch. "Is that store by your house open?"

"I think so."

"Does it have fresh vegetables?"

"Yeah."

In a few minutes, Kay and Claire had left the noise and lights of Yonge Street behind and were passing by the university. Kay turned north on St. George Street.

"Where're you going?" Claire asked, waving her hand to indicate the street in front of her. "It's faster if you go along College."

"I know, but I don't want to run into Jordan."

Claire rolled her eyes and stuck out her tongue, but briefly, then shrugged. "Okay."

Halfway up the block, a dark-haired woman in a trench coat walked toward them. Claire squinted at the woman, as if she were having a bit of trouble bringing the woman's face into focus, but the woman did not return Claire's glance. Instead her eyes met Kay's for an uncertain moment, then darted away.

"Oh, my God," Claire said when the woman had passed. "She's so beautiful."

Kay nodded. "Yeah. She's an actor-friend of Peggy's. I went to a party at her house once. She lives in the Annex."

"You went to a party at her house? Why didn't you say hi?"

"She wouldn't remember me. It was about a year and a half ago. Before I went to Montreal."

Claire looked at Kay. "You want to get a pizza slice or something?"

"I had a muffin."

"Massimo's is great. You can get a vegetarian."

"I thought you were allergic to cheese."

"I don't think I am anymore. I'm eating yoghurt again. Liz says it goes in cycles."

Kay hesitated for an instant, her stride imperceptibly delayed, before gazing up at the lighted windows of the Robarts Library. The enormous concrete library loomed high above the smaller gothic buildings of the university, its narrow windows resembling the perforations in a computer card. "Did you get some work done on your essay?" Kay asked.

Claire shrugged, showing by her expression that it wasn't something she was too worried about.

"You got an extension?"

"Yuppers."

"You know, Claire," Kay began, closing her eyes. "If you don't do something when you say you're going to do it, no one will take you seriously."

"Are you sure you don't want to get something quick to eat?"

Kay, unsure for the second time in a minute whether she should speak, said nothing.

They walked on Harbord now. Claire was pointing out a lovely verandah when she stopped outside the window of the Caversham Bookstore. "Shit," she said, pointing at a book in the window. "I keep forgetting to buy that book." Kay stood on the sidewalk and watched Claire slide her gloved finger along the snowy window ledge. There was a long list of words on the glass near the door:

PSYCHOANALYSIS
PSYCHOTHERAPY
PSYCHIATRY
PSYCHOLOGY
COUNSELLING
SELF-HELP

BOOKS
ON
DREAMS
DEATH
DIVORCE

OBSESSION
DEPRESSION
PARANOIA

NEUROSIS
PSYCHOSIS

GRIEF
ANXIETY
PANIC

ADOLESCENCE
TUMESCENCE

ANOREXIA
DYSLEXIA

DRUGS
VIOLENCE
INCEST
ABUSE

ALCOHOLISM
HOMELESSNESS
OLD AGE
STRESS

SEXISM
FETISHISM
TERRORISM

Kay was halfway through reading this list when someone on a bicycle sped by and yelled hello at Claire. Kay turned to see who it was but the cyclist had already disappeared into the traffic on Spadina Avenue.

"Patrick's squash partner," Claire said, turning away from the bookstore and tugging again on her sock. "I forget his name. He's in law school."

It was ten after eight when Kay and Claire arrived with two bags of groceries at Claire's house. Claire lived on the second floor of a brick Victorian house on Palmerston Avenue, just north of Harbord. Her entrance was through the back door.

"That's a joke, right?" Kay was saying as she followed Claire along the narrow walkway beside the house. "You're joking, right? You didn't really do it."

"He explained it to me. I can show it to you on paper. It works exponentially. You see, if you get five people in it and they each pay a thousand dollars—"

"Aside from everything else," Kay said, "they're illegal."

"Yeah, because people don't pay taxes is why. Jeff's friend made four thousand dollars in three weeks!"

"No, because—because where does the money come from? Where does all the money come from, Claire? Really what they're doing is taking money from their friends."

"No," said Claire, flicking open the gate latch. "Because they'll make their money just like the people on the top. It's like the base of the pyramid just gets bigger."

"It doesn't work, Claire. Trust me. Eventually they fall apart and you lose your money."

"This one's been going for seven years, Kay."

"Claire," Kay said, touching her hand to her eyes, as though the conversation had suddenly become unendurable. "Claire, please don't do it. You don't have the money. Those things are really stupid, and you'll just lose all your money."

Claire took out her keys. "I already told Tasha I'd pay five hundred."

"Tell her you don't want to do it anymore. Tell her you don't have the money."

"Okay," Claire said. "I already said I'd do it, though. And she's just going to say that I can always get together a few hundred dollars. She'll probably just get someone else and they'll make all my money now."

"Claire—" Kay said. And then stopped.

Nodding, as if she were going to think very closely about this later, Claire opened the door, kicked off her boots, and explaining that she really had to pee, ran upstairs to the apartment.

Left alone, Kay bent down and removed her Beatle boots and placed them neatly near the door. Then she leaned over and wiped away the salty slush from the toe of Claire's cowboy boot. Other footwear lay in disordered little heaps along the side of the stairs. As Kay walked up the steps in her stockinged feet, she noticed a burgundy-coloured loafer, a pair of yellow sailing boots, black high-heel shoes, red canvas sneakers, and, beside a leopard fur beret, a single Birkenstock sandal. There was a lingering odour of cigarettes and hairspray in the air; coming to Claire's apartment always reminded Kay of getting her hair cut.

"Where's the Globe-Wernicke bookshelf?" Kay said, pausing at the top of the stairs to look down the hall. Hanging on the wall was a blue painting she hadn't seen before.

"What?" shouted Claire from inside the bathroom.

"The bookshelf with the glass doors." Kay went over to look at the painting.

"It's at Patrick's."

"But it's Grandy's."

"She gave it to me."

"Yeah, but it's only yours to keep not give away."

"I'm going to get it back, Kay. I just have to get the rest of my stuff from Patrick, that's all. I'm living in about three different places right now. I mean, God, I was incredibly lucky that Liz and Tasha still needed someone. And I couldn't afford a mover."

"I forgot to send Grandy a birthday card."

"I sent her an essay from first term. I thought it would be interesting. She probably never reads stuff like that."

"Did she read it?"

"She sent me a thank-you card."

Kay bent down and picked up a fine notice from the University of Toronto Library addressed to Claire. She put it in her pocket. "So, where are your pals?"

"Liz and Tasha? I don't know. Tasha's always at Jeff's. She's so anorexic. You should see her. She practically has to wear paperweights to keep from blowing away."

"Is she really anorexic?"

"I don't know. I don't think so. But she certainly eats a lot of mushrooms. That's all she eats. Mushrooms and crackers. And popcorn."

"How's Liz?"

"I don't know. Not great."

"Did she get her funding?"

"She hasn't heard yet. She's working really hard, she's never here. I'm serious. She's not. She's never here."

For a moment, as she examined the blue painting, Kay felt the tension between the three room-mates, the complex sympathies and criticisms, the invisible boundaries, the ghosts. They would last another year together, Kay thought, maybe two, but no more. She peered at the painting's illegible signature, then continued down the hall to Claire's bedroom. "Is Liz getting along with Tasha?" Kay raised her voice so Claire, still in the bathroom, could hear her.

"Oh yeah. Tasha's really smart. She lived in Senegal for a year."

Kay stood now in Claire's bedroom doorway. The room had been newly painted a glowing salmon colour with gold trim, though the paint stopped halfway around the cornice, leaving the leftover cornice and the room's only window-frame a yellowish-white. A diaphanous silk scarf was pinned across the lower half of the window, and through it Kay could see past a tree and into the bedroom of the neighbouring house.

"Claire," Kay said, "do you want my old curtains?" There was no answer. Kay walked into the centre of the bedroom and looked around. The room was, by Claire's standards, medium-messy. The bed was made but there were papers, opened library books, an abused-looking telephone, and two damp towels strewn across it. Yesterday's clothes—a short black dress, a cotton scarf, black tights, a black bra—lay crumpled on the floor next to the bed. Haphazard on the floor were three ornate wooden picture frames that, Kay remembered, had been purchased at a yard sale the previous summer and which, presumably, Claire was going to fill up with mirrors or photographs. Not far from the frames was a tape player and a pile of cassettes, some in cases, most not. On the other side of the room was a bookshelf made from painted planks and cinder blocks. Beside the shelf and beneath the window a horizontal wooden door rested on stacks of plastic milk crates. On this door were dispersed more books and papers, a Macintosh computer, pencils and pens, and three mugs filled with old coffee. The Macintosh had been a gift from their mother and father. Rather, their mother and father had bought an elaborate Macintosh for Claire, on the condition that she pay back half the cost. The repayment had become complicated, however, when Claire sold this first computer for a cheaper Macintosh with an external hard drive. Where Claire now stood in this transaction, Kay didn't know.

Kay walked over to the desk and peered at the computer screen. The screen-saver was shooting little bursts of fireworks in random patterns. Kay reached down and pressed the return key.

"Hey," Kay called to Claire. "What's this on your computer?"

"What?" came Claire's voice.

"This thing with the bouncing diamond. Crystal Quest."

A stifled scream came from the bathroom. "Oh that. It's just some spazzy game Tasha gave me. It's stupid. Don't worry about it. You just have to set a high score and then it won't bug you anymore."

Kay pressed the return key again and a list of high scores appeared. The first few names were Tasha, Tasha, Tasha, Henley, B-boy, Bob, and i-win. Claire's name appeared at positions seventeen, eighteen and twenty-two. Kay looked at a few of the books on Claire's desk. There were two on art history, a new Penguin paperback of *Bleak House*, *Women in Pakistan*, a dictionary of goddesses, a hardcover with Marilyn Monroe on the cover and a *Sassy* magazine. Kay was picking up the Penguin, examining its unbroken binding, when she heard the toilet flush.

"Claire," Kay said absently. "What's your essay about?"

"The death of the subject."

"What's that?"

"Oh, well, you know, it's like there's no free will, and you think you're making choices but really they're determined by cultural practices and your environment and there's really no overall agency that informs everything."

"I thought it was about India."

"It is. Well, I have a bunch of essays that kind of overlap. The one I'm writing now's about the feminist movement in India. But I'm sort of combining an examination of traditional Indian conventions like suttees and widow's rights and female circumcision with a post-modern interpretation of gender and autonomy." There was a pause. "I've got all reading week to write it."

Kay turned to the computer again. The bouncing diamond was under attack by two glutinous blobs. She leaned closer to watch, and then, abruptly, she stood up straight, undid her coat and laid it along with her scarf and gloves on Claire's bed. She left the room.

"Are you all right?" Kay asked, standing outside the closed bathroom door.

"Fuck," said Claire. "I'm a total spastic."

Kay opened the door. Claire was standing in front of the

sink, staring into the mirror and holding one of her eyelids away from her eye. On Claire's left wrist, a colourful but worn friendship bracelet, a remnant from Mexico, had fallen down her forearm.

"Okay, these contacts are bugging me now," Claire said. Widening her eyes and opening her mouth, she turned to look at Kay. "I think they're in the wrong frigging eyes."

Kay watched Claire bend her head back to drip some saline solution into her left eye. "Who did that painting?" she asked.

Claire widened her eyes again and blinked. Some saline dripped off her face onto the turned-up collar of her leather jacket. "The blue, paint-splashy one? Isn't it great? I got it from this groovy painter-guy, Bob. He used to be a physicist."

Kay stood and watched Claire turn her left eyelid inside out. "Have you read your Christmas present yet?"

Claire, still looking in the mirror, made a clicking noise with her tongue. "I hate Dickens' women characters. He can't write them. And all that anti-semitic stuff ..."

"Who said that, Liz? Well, you might like it anyway. I think it's the best one," said Kay. Turning away, she asked, "Is anyone else home?"

"No. Why?"

"I thought I heard someone."

"Probably just Lilith—Tasha's cat."

Kay nodded and walked to the kitchen.

"Holy Mother of God!" cried Claire.

"What?"

"A squirrel just ran past the window at about a hundred miles an hour."

The kitchen was worse than Claire's room. On the counter beside the sink were five wine glasses half-filled with stale red wine, an overturned bowl of guacamole, an unwinding cassette tape, an ash-filled wine bottle and a pack of Marlboro Lights. A cereal bowl, three spoons and a burnt pot soaked in the sink.

To all of this, Kay's expression remained unchanged. Patiently, mindfully, she went about draining the sink, emptying the glasses, washing the dishes, wiping the counters and generally putting the kitchen to rights.

After a little while, a grey, healthy-looking cat hurried into the kitchen. Kay bent down to lightly scratch behind the cat's ear. Then she stood up and put her hand on the refrigerator. Attached to the door by a plastic cauliflower magnet was a four-page phone bill. At the top of the first page, the three room-mates' names were written in pink hi-liter and after Claire's name was the circled sum of $245.98. Checking this amount against the other two totals, Kay opened the fridge. An envelope of Ilford photographic paper had fallen into a salad bowl filled with left-over fettucini. Kay pressed her lips together and, after a half-hearted scan of the shelves and racks, closed the door. She went to one of the grocery bags and took out a tin of chicken-flavoured cat food. The cat walked in circles at her feet, not exactly purring but making a growly murmur in her throat. Kay opened the tin and spooned some of the food onto a newly washed plate. She set the plate on the floor and picked up the bowl of old water. She emptied this into the sink, refilled it with fresh water and put it down beside the plate of food.

A few minutes later, Claire came in, inspecting her hair for split ends. "You being a kitchen fascist now, Kay?" she asked, watching Kay cut up some green peppers.

"Is this your sharpest knife?"

Claire glanced at the knife and nodded. Then she sat down at the pine table, tucking her right foot under her left thigh, and opened a *Vanity Fair*. After a few seconds, she said,

"Do you know what Liz said about—"

"Oh my God," said Kay. She stopped cutting the green pepper and sniffed. She sniffed again. "What is that? Did you just put perfume on?"

"No. Why?"

"Because I'm allergic to it, whatever it is." Kay pressed her eyes shut and used the hand that was holding the knife to rub at her forehead. "Wow, I'm getting a wicked headache behind my left eye."

"It's probably from the magazine."

Kay bent over the pages and inhaled. "It is," she said. "It's the Eternity ad right there."

"I didn't know you were allergic to that," said Claire, closing the magazine. "I thought it was just that Yardley stuff Mom wears."

The phone on the wall rang.

"Can you get that?" Claire asked. "Because I don't want—"

It rang again.

Kay was filling a pot of water for the rice. "Just a second," she said.

Claire gave Kay a quick forget-it-I'll-get-it look and picked up the phone.

"Hello?" she said, looking at Kay. "Oh, hi. No, that's okay." Claire's expression was mock-dismay, as if she thought that at any second she would be needing help. "Well, actually, I'm in the middle of dinner and Kay's here so I should … my sister. No, it was sold out. Older. Sure, yeah. I'll tell her." Claire laughed, as if remembering something pleasant.

Kay popped a piece of green pepper in her mouth and picked up the ginger.

"Get *out*," Claire said. "Get out of here. Wow, that's so brilliant. Even a group show's still really great. You must be so … um-um-um, I don't know. But yeah, sure, we could sort of maybe get together. Oh, when is that? No, I really want to go to that. It's just, um … He said that? That's sweet. Oh, absolutely, absolutely, but I have so much work right now and I should probably start getting stuff done. So anyway I don't know, so yeah, maybe I'll call you at the beginning of next week. Yeah. I will. Okay. Okay. Okay, bye." Claire put the phone back on the hook and groaned.

"Who was that?" Kay asked, pulling out a wok from the cupboard under the sink.

"Do you know what a tesseract is?" Claire asked, and before Kay could respond, Claire said, "Hold on," and began staring intently at the refrigerator door. She stood stock-still. "I'm trying to remember a dream I had … *pish*. Whatever it was is gone out of my head. I seriously can't remember what I was going to say." She touched her temple with the tip of her index finger, then watched Kay wipe the inside of the wok with a paper towel. "You have to wait for the wok to get really hot with that one … Fuck!" she said suddenly, as if she had been stung or bitten. She moved a hand to cover her left eye.

"What now?"

"Fuck."

"*What?*"

"What time does that clock in the hall say?"

Kay looked behind her. "Eight-thirty."

"Fuck. I hate these fucking contacts. I think I have them in wrong."

"So wear your glasses," Kay said.

Claire blinked a few times and, reassured that her contacts were functioning properly, said, "Sorry Kay. That was that guy, Bob. He says to say hi."

"The guy who gave you the painting?"

"Yeah. He gave it to me for Valentine's and now he won't stop phoning. It's driving me crazy."

"Why?"

"Oh, I don't know. I kind of have this ridiculous relationship with him. I act like a child. But the problem is, he has an enormous crush on me."

Kay turned on a gas element and looked at Claire. "One of your pilot lights is out. Did you sleep with him?"

"You should see him," Claire said, as if confessing. "He's beautiful. He's one of the most beautiful men I know."

"Another one?" said Kay, arranging the cut mushrooms, green peppers, celery, onion, and garlic for transfer to the wok. "You seem to know a lot of beautiful men."

Shrugging, as if she were considering this for the first time, Claire slid across the floor and took an opened bag of chocolate chips from the cupboard. She put a fingerful in her mouth. "Bob wants me to go out with him after the opening of his show."

"Are you going to?"

"I'm supposed to be seeing a lecture with Patrick that night."

Kay stopped. "You're still seeing Patrick?"

Claire nodded, chewing.

"You're *seeing* him? Claire. Why? It's just going to screw things up."

"He kept calling me. So I told him we had a few options. We could completely stop seeing each other; we could see each other but not sleep together; or we could sleep together but not see each other. With blindfolds." Claire laughed and scratched at her cheek. "And anyway, Liz says that you sleep with people three times after you break up. Didn't you do that with Jordan?"

"Twice," said Kay, not missing a beat. She poured a bit of olive oil into the wok. "Well, what about this guy, Bob? Do you like him?"

"Sort of. He's nice. But I mean, I don't want to spend the rest of my life with him or anything like that. He's too obsessive." Claire watched Kay lift up the bowl of onions. The hot wok hissed as Kay spooned in the onions and garlic, splattering the hot oil. Kay pushed the onions around with the wooden spoon.

"I mean, why get pinned down?" Claire said, cupping her hand under her left breast and jiggling it softly. "I won't be twenty-four forever. And plus I really love men right now. I mean, I love being with them. And I don't mind sleeping with them. Especially when they're beautiful. I mean, I'm trying to do that as much as I can, just about. And, I don't know, you can't let stuff bother you. You've just got to be honest as much as you can. That's why I told Patrick if he shows up here he's just getting fucked, that's it, and not to expect anything."

"That's fair. As long as it's all safe."

"Patrick always uses condoms. He can't stand the feeling of skin surrounding him. It makes him claustrophobic."

"God, he's weird," Kay said after a moment. She rested her hands on either edge of the stove. "I mean, I always knew he was an asshole, but I didn't think he was such a weirdo."

"That's a pretty snotty thing to say, Kay, if you think about it. You don't even know him. And he's not a weirdo. He's just—he's just like a normal guy with problems."

"Claire, *rapists* are just normal guys with problems." Kay looked straight at Claire, then added the rest of the vegetables to the wok. As they hit the hot metal, the outer-edges of the oil made a shrieking sound. Kay turned the gas down and mixed in a handful of chopped ginger. "Does this guy Bob know about Patrick or Henley?"

"No. Come on, you can't be honest about everything. I told him … well, I sort of told him about it. I mean what guy would be thrilled to learn about the other guys? Bob and I aren't in a relationship or anything. Life is so … I mean you have to enjoy things. I don't want to get to the end of my life and—and not have experienced anything. Besides, I can tell he doesn't want to know."

"Well, does Henley know about the other two?"

"Oh yeah. Henley's like an old-fashioned cool boy. It's good for him just to sleep with me and not have a relationship. I mean, he had the same girlfriend for four years. Now he just wants it to be easy. He knows I sleep with other people, but he doesn't know the details. That's why I introduced him to Pru."

There was a pause.

"Okay," Kay said. "Who's Pru?"

"Oh, this lesbian of colour Henley and I know."

Kay was silent.

"We were all out one night and went home together."

"Who did?"

"Henley and—"

"Henley was *there*? The three of you went home?"

"Look, Kay, there's no need to get so uptight. It was fine."

"How long have you been sleeping with women?"

"Pru's the first. I just decided I'd do it. I think it's important. I mean, I could be a lesbian."

"Claire—you don't just *decide* you're going to be a lesbian."

"How do you know?"

"Well, I don't know, Claire. But it doesn't seem like the type of thing you just decide out of the blue. Just like that. I don't know if you just rush out and sleep with women to, to—"

"Why not? That's what happened to Pru. She just decided it made more sense. And it made her feel better."

"Pru? That's her name?"

"Not really, no. Her real name's Sharon."

"Oh for fuck's sake." Kay stopped stirring and, as if nine years of city life had finally become too much for her, looked squarely at Claire. "Then why do you call her Pru?"

"Because she changed her name to Pruey."

"Oh, come on, Claire."

"Lots of people change their name, Kay. Grammy Jean changed her name."

"Yeah, but Grammy Jean was named after a *province*," Kay said, laughing as she spoke. She closed her eyes, took a deep breath and resumed stirring.

"Anyway, Pru's gorgeous," said Claire. "She's really beautiful. I used to follow her around the university before I met her. And she can look so ugly. That's the real criterion. She has the greatest red hair."

"A lesbian of colour with red hair?"

"Well, that's it exactly. That's her colour."

"Claire," Kay said, "for Christ's sake. That's ridiculous. Some people would take a lot of offence at that."

"Maybe. Actually, technically, she's more of an orangey, marmalade colour, a carrot-top. Whereas you're more chestnutty. Although when you were a kid I guess I would have called it red."

"When you were a kid you did call me carrot-top."

"Yeah, but when I was five you and Jill Keating told me I was really twenty but I was mentally retarded and had the mental age of a five year old."

Kay looked into the wok and laughed. "Did we?"

"Yes. And then you blindfolded me and told me you were taking me to the group home on Maple Street." Claire opened the refrigerator, looked in one of the drawers, and brought out a long, green stringy vegetable. From behind Kay's shoulder, she dropped it in the wok.

"What're you doing?" Kay asked, alarmed.

"I don't think there's enough flavour in there personally. And this is really good."

"What is it?"

"Hijiki."

"What is it? It looks like seaweed."

"It is. You get it at this great little store in Chinatown."

Kay watched as the hijiki mixed into the other vegetables. "You and your purple soups," she said. "Have you applied to art college yet? Do you think you'll get in?"

Claire swallowed a few more chocolate chips. "I don't know. I mean, if I get in great, and if I don't, whatever. I mean you can't hinge your life on one thing."

"Yeah, but you can't hinge your life on whatever."

"Well, I applied to a few other places, too."

"Where?"

Claire moved her tongue around her back teeth, loosening some sticking chocolate. "You know, Kay, I can only handle this guidance-counsellor routine for so long."

"I know there's something to be said for living life as it comes, but I don't think you can just—"

"The rice is burning." Claire, holding the bag of chocolate chips in one hand, pointed to the rice pot with the other. Thick vapours of steam escaped from beneath the pot's tight-fitting lid. Claire watched Kay turn down the gas. "It's just that there has to be more to life that than sitting around and obsessing about work," Claire said, taking out a bottle of red wine from the shelf on the refrigerator door. She took two of the wine glasses that Kay had washed and put them on the table. "There has to be. I mean, look how fucked up this TV show is making your life. Does one stupid review really matter that much? I mean, how much will you care about it in ten years?"

Kay peeked inside the rice pot. "I don't know. I go crazy when I'm not doing anything, Claire. You know that. I feel like I don't have the right to be here."

"You've been here too long if you feel like that," Claire said. "Though I can understand it."

Kay watched Claire pour the wine. "The show will probably get cancelled anyway," she said, abstracted. "And all it really means is that I won't be able to take taxis or eat in restaurants anymore. And I love eating in restaurants because I always feel thirty-three in a restaurant." Kay gave Claire a quick, unqualified smile. "Maybe I just need to get laid."

"Bingo," Claire said, and laughed. She took a sip of wine and stood up. She had unbuttoned her skirt and unzipped it a little. A swell of pink belly pushed over the skirt's waistband. Claire put her hand under her shirt and absently rubbed her stomach. "What about your script? How's Maya? Have you figured out what to do with her yet?"

"It's hard to work and write at the same time," Kay said, looking at Claire's belly. "You look huge."

"I know. My breasts, too. Look. Rock-solid boobs. They're really sore. I can't wait till I get my period. Will told me to tell you to finish it. Your script, I mean. He said the sooner you write it the better. Are you going to get him to play Marvin?" Claire inhaled and pushed her stomach out further, her skin stretching to expose the blotchy pink spots of white skin in winter. "Actually," she said, "I told Liz that Will offered me a job."

"Did he?"

"No. Don't be stupid. I'm fourteen years old in his eyes. He thinks I'm a dinky little girl. But Liz would love to think that he offered me a job."

Kay looked at Claire, a little amazed. "Have you told anyone else?"

"About the job?"

"About being late."

Claire looked at Kay as if she weren't sure what Kay was talking about. Then she pulled up her skirt's zipper and slid over to the table. Nodding, she picked up the almost-empty bag of chocolate chips and said, "Oh, I don't think I'm pregnant anymore. I'm just having these crazy cuckoo hormones. They're all messed up from not getting enough sleep and from playing squash. Liz had the same thing happen when she was finishing her Masters. She was two months late because she didn't get enough sleep."

"Claire, you're being ridiculous. Just go see a doctor."

"I don't need to see a doctor. And what's he going to do, anyway? Give me an antibiotic?"

"Well, if you don't want to see a doctor, just go to a drugstore. Or buy a home pregnancy test."

"Well then I'm pregnant, because it's blue."

"You mean you did one? Was it the first morning's pee?"

"There was one in our bathroom. I think it was Sabina's."

"But she moved out two years ago!"

"So? It would still work, wouldn't it?"

"Claire," Kay said. "Do you really think you're pregnant, yes or no?"

"*No*," Claire said, as if the question required no thought at all. "Do you?"

"You're not throwing up in the morning or anything like that, are you?"

"No," Claire said, dismissing the notion as absurd and sounding in that moment, they both knew, like their mother.

"Look, you can't fool around with something like this, that's all. The longer you let it go, the worse it gets. It's not something you can put off."

"Don't you think I would know if I was pregnant? My body would be able to feel it." Claire took a drink of wine. "Is that what you've been talking about all day with your psychiatrist? What did she tell you?"

"She doesn't tell me anything. She just points things out."

"Well, did she point out that you might be more upset about this than I am? Did she point out that it might be harder for you than it is for me? Did she point out that you turn everything into a problem?"

"I'm just a little wor—"

"Jesus Christ, Kay. Just stop it. Worry about something else. Worry about your stupid review. But don't worry about me. Worry about your fucking shrink."

The telephone rang. Claire looked at Kay, then said she'd

get it in the other room. Kay sat down and waited at the table. After a while, she took the rice pot off the stove. Balancing the wooden spoon on the edge of the sink, she poured the rice into a large hand-painted bowl. Then she spooned the rice onto two plates, poured the steaming sauce from the wok over each, and sat down again. She crossed her legs. Then she uncrossed them to reach across the table to pull the tablecloth so it was centred properly. Then she called to Claire that the dinner was ready.

At about twenty after ten, when they had finished eating, Kay said that she had to get up early the next day and should get going.

"You can have that *Vanity Fair* if you want, Kay," Claire said. "I'm finished reading it."

Kay, standing up, said that it was okay, she didn't need it. She went and got her things from Claire's bed, and remembering that Claire hadn't yet returned the white blouse she'd borrowed some months ago, Kay asked if she could get it back. Claire, leaning against the doorway, holding her cup of coffee, explained that it was being dry-cleaned. Kay gave a last look at Claire's stomach, buttoned her coat, and kissed Claire twice on the cheek. Lilith the grey cat skittered over the hardwood floor and dashed down the stairs. "It's okay," Claire said, "she's allowed out."

Kay asked Claire if she needed any money.

"No, I'm okay, thanks," Claire said, brushing some hair away from her eye.

"But what about your bank machine?"

"Oh. Oh yeah."

Kay took two twenty-dollar bills from her pocket and gave them to Claire.

"Thanks, Kay."

Kay went down the stairs, careful not to trip over any shoes. Claire sat on the top step, watching Kay guide her feet into her boots. Kay waved to Claire and then, letting the cat go out in front of her, left the house.

Once outside, Kay walked down the dark walkway to the sidewalk. She looked briefly toward Bloor Street and then, for whatever reason, began walking very briskly toward Harbord. Suddenly, a woman on a bicycle without a light came around the corner on the sidewalk, and Kay had to hop off the curb and into a gutter full of slush to dodge her, soaking her left foot through to the skin.

She was looking to hail a cab on Harbord Street when she heard the sounds of someone whimpering. A young man was sitting on the curb beside a No Parking sign. Attached to the sign by a kryptonite lock was an abandoned and misshapen bicycle wheel, its spokes bent and broken. The man's face was buried in his hands. Apart from a day or two's growth of beard, he appeared to be well cared for.

After a moment's hesitation, Kay asked him if he were all right. The man held his sobs to himself for a moment and nodded. Then he began coughing. Kay asked him again if he were okay or if he needed anything. The man shook his head. He wanted to be left alone.

Kay scuffed the toe of her dry boot into some clean snow on the curb and watched a taxi go by. She watched another taxi go by. She took a last look at the young man then crossed Harbord and resumed walking south. She was thinking she would take the College streetcar.

She made a little jump over the grey slush on someone's driveway and looked at the sidewalk ahead of her. Some of it was cleanly shovelled and salted, some patchily shovelled, and some not shovelled at all, with packed-down, walked-on snow.

It wasn't supposed to snow again tonight, though, Kay remembered. The clouds had cleared. She looked up to a full moon in the sky. Strange, Kay thought, you never really keep track of the phases of the moon, yet one night you look up into the sky to see a sudden full moon. She remembered the blue moon she'd seen in Ottawa last year, when she and Claire had walked home from the Parliament Hill celebrations on New Year's Eve. Walking across another intersection, Kay drew her coat closer to her neck, though only her soaked foot was cold, and watched her shadows on the sidewalks. She drew a certain comfort from the sober order of the evenly spaced Palmerston streetlamps, their round bulbs haloed in light or obscured by a few bare tree branches. Kay sighed and watched again as her shadow accelerated beneath her, watched it stretch, fade, then finally disappear as the next lamp began another shadow behind her.

Opening Night

MIDNIGHT AND UNDERNEATH the trestle of the Dupont railway tracks Will slips and falls on the black ice. He springs up, unhurt, brushes the snow from his jeans. Snow everywhere, like dirty mashed potatoes, in the street, piled on sidewalks, collecting in clunky lumps behind car tires. He walks down Howland Avenue, picking his way over frozen slush. All these streets, Howland, Albany, Brunswick, Barton, left over from another era. Stately Victorian houses, brick turrets and gabled roofs. Cut up into apartments now, storm windows replaced by metal frames, fireplaces filled with flowers, decks added and removed ... Students, professors, gay couples, journalists, writers. Canadian culture out walking the dog. Rodney's friend who renovates houses. Joel? Will looks up, a few stars scattered across the cold night sky. Jason? No, he can't remember. So long since he's paid attention to anything outside the play. He's still a little worried about one of the actors. Her performance different every night and twice during tonight's preview she forgot her lines. Too late now. Best thing to do is keep up morale.

Will turns onto Bloor Street where some drunken men leave the Brunswick House Tavern They scrum toward him, wearing only T-shirts, their bare arms around each other, chanting:

—Go-Jethro-Go-Jethro-Go! Go-Jethro-Go-Jethro-Go!

Drunk students horsing around, making people nervous.

—Go-Jethro-Go-Jethro-Go! Go-Jethro-Go-Jethro-Go!

A woman in front of Will stiffens, crosses the street. Will looks ahead as the men pass, their laughter receding. The laughter of men. Will looks in the window of By The Way Café. Home again, home again, clickety-clack. He hasn't seen Mikey in weeks. A lone patron sits in the window, a guy with a goatee and a book by Umberto Eco. They come from far to grow goatees, and sip at night their herbal teas. Punish the world with poetries. Dhotis. Capotes ... Oh there's Mikey, the cutest waiter, long hair falling over his eyes, carrying a teapot and cup. Will presses his face against the window, closes his eyes to kiss the glass. Gorgeous Mikey drops a spoon. Umberto Eco turns a page.

Will about to go home instead runs to Bloor SuperSave, all-night grocery. He asks for hockey cards, the new series. A treat for Stephano who collects them. Three-fifty a pack, not even gum anymore, just smiley guys with bad haircuts, short in the front, long in the back, the great Canadian hockey haircut. Steph obsessed since arriving in Canada. Five Patrick Roys.

All the lights on in the apartment and Will wants Steph home, a sneaking hope that Steph's waiting for him, but opening the door he finds a disappointing no one. Stephano always out, a little star attraction since hitting town. Will surveys the messy rooms. Candy wrappers. Coke cans. Magazines. Life-drawings, sketches. Half-empty bag of salt-and-vinegar chips. Will collects the litter, stuffs it in the garbage beneath the sink. Tenderly picks up sketches from the floor, places them on top of the bookshelf with the new hockey cards. When does Steph work? So many drawings. It's what he wants to do, though. It's why Will likes him. Stephano watching Will's reel, the beer commercial, the insurance voice-over, "War of the Worlds," Steph holding onto the back of Will's chair, terrified. *That will kill you*, he had said, and Will admired his purist streak. The reel. Will must send it to LA, for the film. Call Pam tomorrow when he sets up the comps. What else? Dry-clean tuxedo. Haircut. Kay for lunch. Wine and flowers for cast. The astronaut audition. At the theatre for six ... He flicks on the TV, scans through the channels, leaves it on Letterman with the sound low. Neighbours have phoned. Like they don't wake up Will every Saturday with Supertramp and RUSH. All that stuff he tried to like. Thank God, he doesn't have to be a teenager anymore.

In the bathroom Will swallows an aspirin, massages his face. These long days are ageing him. Looks for the moisturizer. Steph must have finished it. Drinks a glass of water. Flicks off the TV. Sets his alarm for eight-thirty, thinks briefly what he would say to Letterman about his play, then, too tired to masturbate, he falls asleep.

Twelve-thirty the next day and Will hurries across the street to the Senator restaurant, fingering the newly buzzed hair on the back of his neck, remembering from years ago a skinhead, the boy's face on his stomach ... A man in a business suit pauses in thought, his hand on the restaurant door. Looks anonymous, the way Will's mother used to look. To be a businessman ... This one's balding and sunburned and he opens the door and enters, as if he hasn't seen Will, as if Will isn't noticeable. Sure, Will thinks, don't hold the door for me. Try and bring me down and make me feel shitty. The conceit of people bogged down in dailiness.

Inside, the clank of waiters, smell of soups, murmurs of the line-up. Will butts by to look for Kay, Kay who is ... yes, in one of the boothed-in tables at the back, her head down, ignoring two other businessmen at the neighbouring table. A heap of shredded napkin at Kay's fingers, Kay a little compulsive kid picking a knee-scab. Will slides into the other side of the booth, pulls his whistle out of his sweater, leans over to kiss her.

—So where've you been? Kay asks, looking up. I haven't seen you in ages.

—No, I know. No one has. I'm domesticated now. When I'm not at the theatre, me and Steph are home playing Pictionary.

—Oh. Tell Stephano Tasha's not going to buy his camera.

—Tasha? Who's Tasha?

The two suits are joined by the sunburned man. Nose peeling. Jovial greetings.

—Claire's room-mate. I guess she was supposed to buy his camera or something.

Steph selling his camera, he just bought it, didn't he? Don't remember selling it. Crisp white shirt of the waiter. Articulate-but-bored voice. Probably another actor. Will orders.

—How is Claire? Will asks. Is she still having everyone's baby?

—Who knows? We're still fighting. I've talked to her once. She's had a bottle of urine beside her bed for a week but that's it. She's so funny ...

Kay's exasperated woman-against-the-world voice, so pointy.

—Funny weird or funny ha-ha?

—Funny weird. She's all over the map. She's been seeing a slew of different guys lately and the other day she's like, "Kay, what should I do? I sleep with them and they ask me out. What should I do? I don't want to *date* them." And she's dead serious. That's the scary part. She's got toothbrushes all over the city.

—She's just discovering her pussy, Kay. Leave her alone.

Kay finicky with the salt and pepper, the glass ashtray, lining it up, turning it around, spinning it. She sits up straight.

—To tell you the truth, I just hate to see her flirt with assholes.

—*All* young women flirt with assholes, Kay. It's part of their charm.

—It's part of their tragedy. You know, Claire and her friends pay attention to all these different things like movies and crystals and bands and pottery and vitamins and blue-green algae, but I just hope she puts it to better use than taking XTC all weekend and screwing her Tai Chi instructor.

—She's young, Kay. She's only twenty-three.

—She's twenty-four, and she's waifing out. She doesn't have enough money to pay her rent but she spends seventy dollars to get her roots done—and she's like *that* far away from getting a tattoo on her tit.

Kay at the end of her little tour-de-force, staring into Will's eyes, holding up her finger and thumb.

—What kind of tattoo?

—She can't decide. Something vaguely foreign like the I Ching or a copyright symbol.

—On her tit? Will smiles. You give good stress, Kay. But stop being such a bossy cow. That's the style when you're a college-girl feminist and your life is full of angst and quasi-lesbian encounters.

—Oh, that's right, she says. I forgot. Now she thinks it might be nifty to be a lesbian.

—Who doesn't? says Will, watching Kay's fingers. Has she slept with any yet?

—Hm-mm.

—Dyke or straight?

—One of those dykes who sleeps with men.

—That doesn't count. It's not the same.

Kay's fingers returning to the ashtray, spinning it, a series of quarter-turns. Nervous gymnastics.

Will leans back, rubbing the new bristles on the nape of his neck. The sunburned man regaling his pals with his trip to Bangkok.

—Where did Claire see Stephano?

Kay studying her menu, doesn't look up, her hair falling to one side like a curtain.

—I don't know. Out dancing at some club.

Will takes the ashtray from Kay's fingers, drops in the remains of the shredded napkin.

—I talked to Peggy the other day, he says. She's trying to get a new sitcom on. She's pitching it next week.

—Why'd you call her?

—I'm thinking of visiting. She thinks it might be big, this sitcom.

—Jordan's moving to New York in June, she says. PolyGram offered him one of their international marketing positions and he's taking it.

—What happened to his cowboys?

—They were signed by PolyGram. They're going to market them bigtime. They're giving them thirty grand to do a video.

—Wow. Those boys usually play for bar tab ... Any word about "Agenda?"

The waiter arrives with the drinks. Kay leans back.

—Cancelled, she says, I'm sure. It isn't official yet, but it'll happen. Everybody's just waiting. No one's got anything to do.

—What did the gorgeous boss-man say? I thought he loved Angela.

—Oh, he does. I don't know how much control he has, though. There's just no money.

—It's such a heavy word.

—Which?

—Cancelled.

—I know. It kind of makes me sick.

Will squeezes lemon into his water.

—And what about Maya? What she been doing lately?

—Nothing. But I got a really good idea for her the other day.

—Yeah?

—She's going to have a baby.

—You mean she gets impregnated by the UFO?

—Yeah, by Marvin. The homeless guy.

—That's great. That's so perfect. So she's Claire.

—No, Maya's not Claire.

Will sips his water.

—How different's the script now? I didn't realize you'd been working on it so much. Have you changed anything else?

—Not really. I've been working on it at the office because there's nothing else to do.

After lunch, Kay looks at her watch, says she wants to go. They pay the bill and put on their coats. The sunburned man from the neighbouring table squeezes out from his booth, his napkin falling to the floor.

—Kay? Kay Pritchard?

Kay staring. Can't remember his name, you can tell. He's halfway over to her, hand outstretched, wedding band. The other two men stunned the bald guy knows the babe.

—Chris, he says, helping.

—Chris *McGuire*.

—When I saw the red hair I just knew it was you. But I didn't know you were in Toronto. I thought you guys moved to Ottawa.

—My parents did. But I've been here since university. And you?

—Oh, a long time now. Seventy-nine. We just built a new house in Markham. Hey, how come we didn't see you at Jill's wedding?

And Kay does the hometown thing, the conversation you have whenever you run into someone from high school. Who got married, who has babies, who has jobs, who has died, who's been back lately. Mr. Chris McGuire, amiable businessman, healthy but a bit worn. Scrunched suit. And his tie, blue-and-yellow-striped, with a brown houndstooth. These guys never get it right. His eagerness touches Will, how out of place he seems, and yet how pleasant, his willingness to block the aisle, upset the waiters, all to find out what's happening in Kay's life. Mr. McGuire, making a living in Toronto, paying a mortgage, paying taxes, thinking about affairs, not quite a Fuck, not quite a Die. He looks forty years old.

—Chris, Kay says, stepping back. This is my friend Will Weston.

—How are you? Chris McGuire says, shaking hands. Are you in television as well?

—Kind of. I'm an actor, Will says, unable to rid himself of an idiotic polite smile.

—Really ...? Hey, have you guys seen *Phantom*? We saw it last week. Great show. *Great* show.

—Actually, Kay says, Will's directing his first play and it opens tonight.

—Is that right? Chris McGuire says, noticing the whistle around Will's neck. Is that right? That's great ... Hey, Kay, how's that little sister of yours? Is she back down east?

—She's great. She's at U of T.

—My brother Mike still talks about her.

Abruptly, Chris McGuire stops talking. He smiles expectantly. Kay extends her hand.

—Well it was great to see you again, Kay.

Chris McGuire keeps shaking her hand. Finally, he returns to his companions.

—Wow, Will says, walking toward the door. He was so happy to see you.

Kay leans into his ear.

—I gave him a blow job in grade nine and he's still grateful.

Outside, the bright cold afternoon.

—I can't find my suit, Will says, buttoning his coat.

—What suit?

—My tuxedo. I looked all over for it this morning. It's

going to be rumpled now. I wanted to press it for the opening.

—Oh you look so cute in your tuxedo. What's Stephano wearing?

—Oh, I didn't think of that. Maybe Stephano took it to the cleaners.

—How's it going anyway? Kay says, pulling her gloves tight on her hands. She's thinking, smiling a little.

—Fine. We haven't seen much of each other lately. But it'll be better when I'm finished this play.

Kay nods, asks if he wants to see a movie.

—What one?

—Any one. It doesn't matter.

—I'd like to, but I've got an audition at four.

—For what?

—Some astronaut movie. It's really good money.

Kay looks at Will with true surprise, baffled at such auditions, openings, good money, and Will sees that Kay's just tired after all, just worried about losing her job. He takes her hand, walks her up Victoria Street to the doors of the Carlton cinema.

—This is where your movie's going to play, he says. What's the title?

—I don't know, she says, blowing some hair out of her eyes. All I can think of is *Satan's Cunt*.

Will laughs, forgetting Kay likes to surprise him when he's not paying enough attention.

—Very catchy. So really *you're* Maya, then.

—That's right, Kay says, catching his eye. You look like you're on shore leave with that haircut.

—I know.

Will pulls her close for a hug. Kay's chin in his chest. He leans back and lifts her up.

—I know. I look like Dean. It's my astronaut-do.

—Is Dean coming tonight? I haven't seen him in ages either. I haven't seen anybody.

—If he gets his shit together. He lost his date-book so he's been calling all of us to see if we can remember where he put it.

—That's like Claire, Kay says, putting her arms around him. When we were kids, if she forgot something, she thought I'd be able to remember it for her. If I closed my eyes and thought hard enough.

Will pulls her closer.

—I'm on my toes, says Kay. You'll fall over if I let go.

—I know, Will says, releasing her. Have a good movie, Miss Thing. And you are going to wash your hair tonight before you come, aren't you?

Kay snaps him, flicking her wrist. Kay's always unsuccessful attempts to be queenie. Kind of endearing.

—See you tonight, Will says. He goes to a pay phone to check his messages.

Four-forty and Will uneasy in the back of a cab, stopped at a traffic light. He rubs at his face. Audition was good, made them laugh, casting director's always liked him. He thinks he's going to get it. Something bugging him, though. Surprised to see Michael Podowinski there, changed agents probably. Light turns green and the wind, as the cab accelerates, picks up snow and blows it in quick silent spirals. Will wonders where Steph is. Called three times, no answer. Still thinking about it when they reach Brunswick Avenue. Will gathers his things, pays, overtips. Good karma, nice karma, stay karma. A fat old pigeon, along the sidewalk, flaps crookedly ahead. Will circles around it, off the sidewalk. Looking back, he hears his name.

Mrs. Bobkowicz, who runs the second-hand store with her husband, two doors away from the By The Way, leans out of her cracked door, yelling.

—Willy! Willy!

Will comes to the store, asks what's the matter. Mrs. Bobkowicz shakes her head, crosses her wattled arms.

—I said to my husband it's not okay. It's not okay. Why should another man sell it when Will's name's in it?

—Sell what, Will asks, and instantly sneezes, the dust in the store in his throat.

—My husband, your friend came in to sell it to him. But your name is in it and I say, "Why Will want to sell this? It's worth money? It's so nice." But if I didn't buy it someone else would, right?

Will, looking at the tuxedo, asks her how much she paid for it.

—Just sixty dollars.

—He sold it to you for sixty dollars?

—No. He sold it for fifty dollars. But we dry-cleaned it for you.

Her enormous bosom heaving, Mrs. Bobkowicz points to a clothes rack behind the front counter and there on a curved wooden hanger, the tuxedo Will purchased from the Citadel Theatre in Edmonton when he did *Private Lives*.

Soon he is on the stairs to his apartment, unlocking his door, pushing it open. Dark. The blinds pulled shut. Bedroom door closed. More Coke cans on the telephone desk. On the floor, half-eaten O'Henry bars. Shrivelled crescent of pizza crust. Red socks wet beside the sofa, staining the wood floor. Pack of Winston cigarettes. On the coffee table a new issue of FMR.

—Stephano?

Will lays the tuxedo on a chair, his bags on the floor. It's five o'clock.

—Stephano!

His eyes still taking in the room, his gaze stops on two cords dangling from the television.

—Stephano! he yells. Where's my fucking VCR?! He takes a step toward the bedroom, stumbling on a derelict boot, hitting his head on the bookshelf. Sparkly points of light, more stars and then drawings, drawings he picked off the floor last night, drawings he had lovingly placed on the bookshelf, drawings he refuses to see anymore and he flings them at the bedroom door, horses and bulls scattering across the room. More in his hands, he twists them, rips them in half, pitches them at the ceiling. Stephano now standing in the open doorway, naked, rubbing his chest with his left hand, tilting his head upward, watching pieces of his drawings float down to the hardwood floor, settling gently into piles on top his socks, his cigarettes, his chocolate bars.

Bob's Blue Painting

CLAIRE STANDS IN FRONT of Bob's blue painting. She has been staring at it for almost a minute. The blue bean shapes in the centre of the canvas, next to the little green swirls, play in and out of a subtle pattern she hadn't noticed before. It isn't easy to see, because the greens and blues, so close together, create a visual vibration, forcing her eye away from the centre.

It is Friday evening, and she has just spent five hours at Robarts Library preparing a seminar for Monday morning. Happy that she managed to stay so long at the library, she has walked home in the cold, tired but content. She is finally weaning herself of the night-before habit. Liz invited her to a restaurant opening, but Claire has arrived home too late and the apartment is empty. Tasha, presumably, is at her boyfriend's for the weekend, so Claire is alone for the night. She is in studying garb: messy hair, a loose-fitting shirt that exposes a twisted beige bra strap, faded dirty jeans, heavy black tights, and white tube socks, one of which has slipped so far forward that the tip flaps in front of her toes.

Claire leaves off looking at the painting and goes into the bathroom. On her way home she tried to think of the last time she had a bath. Ottawa, she now remembers, one of those nights in the limbo between Christmas and New Year's. And tonight, with all out-of-doors cold and forbidding, a thin frost on the windows, snow upon the roof, and icicles slinking off the eaves-troughs, tonight is perfect for a nice, long, soaking hot bath.

Pushing her sleeves to her elbows, she kneels down beside the tub and arranges the plastic curtain so that it hangs outside.

Grime stains the porcelain where showerers have stood. Claire turns on the hot-water tap, gets the sponge and Ajax powder, and forcefully rubs away the footprints. She scrubs off the bath ring and, after rinsing the tub with cold water, wedges the crumbling rubber plug into the drain. She turns on both taps.

A eucalyptus branch hangs from a nail above the radiator. Claire picks off several leaves, breaks them in half, and drops them into the tub. The green semi-circles toss for a moment in the torrent of incoming water, before eventually wafting to the back. Taking Tasha's brush from behind the sink, she stands in front of the mirror and pulls the brush through her hair, untangling the knots and curls, her face drained of any expression. When she was young she used to wonder what she'd look like as an adult. And here she is, her adult face, round chin, short nose, dyed-blonde hair, naturally wavy but out of condition, and her skin, still young-looking but with an incipient wrinkle, a single, soft horizontal line on her forehead. Small traces of wrinkles under her eyes, too. Her neck still smooth, though. She is inspecting her pupils, trying to make them wider by force of will, when she remembers the story about Kay's first day of high school. Kay was alone in the girl's bathroom, examining her face in the mirror, when two or three grade-twelve girls came in to smoke. Kay told Claire later that she'd become very flustered at being caught looking in the mirror, and, for whatever reason, Claire has never forgotten this. It is one of those obscure, unnoteworthy details whose persistence, among so many competing memories, surprises Claire, for every other time she looks into a mirror she thinks of Kay's first day of high school.

Claire undresses as she waits for the tub to fill, piling her clothes beside the already-full wicker hamper. She sits naked on the toilet and picks up her book from the radiator. The book is *Bleak House*, and Claire is almost finished. She read about fifty pages in the library earlier in the day, during a break from studying, and still fresh in her mind is the worry that Lady Dedlock is going to die—is, in fact, going to kill herself.

She reads two more pages. Then, checking the temperature of the water with an outstretched toe, lays the book down and turns off the taps. She leans over the tub to fully test the water with her hand. It seems all right, but when she sinks in her left foot, the water feels much hotter and stings the skin around her ankle. After a few seconds, unable to keep her foot submerged, she lifts it out.

She kneels down, turns on the cold water tap, holds her hand under the running water, and swishes the bath water around, the cool of the porcelain tickling her underarm. The overhead light dims for an instant as the furnace comes on below and Claire realizes that, though she is alone in the apartment, she has forgotten she may not be alone in the house. Feeling oddly self-conscious, she quickly stands and steps into the bath. The temperature seems fine now, endurable and so, with a hand on either side of the tub, Claire lowers herself into the hot water, carefully, inch by inch, the tip of her bum touching first, then her thighs, until her weight settles on the bottom, her pale wintry skin reddening, marking a scarlet border around her waist. She straightens her legs and watches the water close over her knees.

Claire sits like this for a minute, gauging the water's heat, before splashing water on her arms and chest. Then she bends her knees up out of the water and slides her body toward the front of the tub. She lies back, her hair spreading across the surface. A drop falls from the faucet and Claire moves to catch it with her toe.

She closes her eyes and thinks of Bob's painting. Maybe she should hang it in her bedroom ... She shivers. The water doesn't seem as hot now. She lifts her right foot and turns on the hot water. As she feels the heat swirl toward her body, she brings her left foot out of the water, too. Soon the bath is full and Claire's slightest movement spills water into the overflow drain. But it is, finally, properly hot and, with steam rising from her knees, Claire turns off the tap and lies back again. The water ebbs just below her chin. She takes the face cloth that was jammed into the soap dish and dips it in the water. Holding it by two corners, she lifts the steaming cloth and lays it across her face. She remains inert in the tub, smelling the faint traces of eucalyptus, until the face cloth loses its heat. A piece of dried black soap no bigger than a quarter lies nudged in the corner by the wall. Claire grips it with her fingernails and separates it from the porcelain. She rubs the soap back and forth until a grey creamy foam appears in her palms. Slipping the soap back into its corner, she smooths the cream across her brow, around her eyes, and down her cheeks to her chin. She leaves it a minute before firmly wiping it off with the face cloth. Then she sits up, runs some cold water into her cupped hands, and splashes it across her face.

Where is the other soap, the glycerin soap? Did it fall in the tub when she took the face cloth? She gropes around the tub, trying to locate it. There it is, she feels it beneath her left thigh. She grabs at it, once, twice, then closes her left hand around it and soaps her stomach, her arms and breasts, between her legs, the soap foaming through her pubic hair, creating what looks to Claire like rice vermicelli or gossamer alfalfa sprouts. She glides her middle finger through the folds of her sex, washing back and forth along her perineum. It's funny for her to think that she can get pregnant. Until now, she has always thought of it as a rumour. She's surprised it hasn't happened before though, and, considering that she hasn't been perfect in her habits, to be pregnant now seems almost inevitable.

There is a slight scratching at the door, two bumps, and Lilith invades the room. She sniffs at the heap of clothes before soundlessly jumping onto the side of the bath-tub. She pokes her head toward the bath water, her tail curling, and then, attentively, fitfully, stretches a paw toward Claire's wet knee. Claire flicks a few drops of water and watches the cat shrink away. Lilith notices Claire's floating hair, looks at the ceiling, and then, as if suddenly reminded of what lies outside the bathroom, she meows and drops to the floor. Claire watches her pad away and slip into the hallway.

Claire reaches for her book. Keeping it well above the water, she begins to read. But her arms soon tire, and she sees that the book's binding is starting to swell in the steam, so after finishing the next paragraph, she puts it down again. Her hands are furrowed and beaded with little drops of sweat. The bridge of her nose, too, feels itchy with perspiration. Claire tries to will the itchiness away. She wrinkles her nose. She opens her mouth. Finally, she wets her hands and massages her face. She runs her tongue across her teeth. They feel rough and unclean.

Claire holds her breath and forces her stomach above the water, making little rivers stream off her belly. How round and full her stomach feels. Her nipples, too, seem larger. She cups a hand around each breast and gathers them together. It's true, she has felt vaguely uncomfortable about missing her period, it's as if she's failed a test, but more and more, after considering the possibilities, she feels composed about it. She wants to have babies. She was thinking yesterday how she wants to knit them sweaters, attend their music recitals, read them *The Happy Prince*, even though the story of the swallow would make them cry, perhaps because it would make them cry. And she doesn't want to wait until she's thirty-eight. She doesn't want to be an old mom with bad teeth.

She exhales, letting her stomach sink below the water, and watches the water fill her belly-button. And it is, after all, still very possible she would have her period. The symptoms are so similar. But her shape really has been changing, her breasts feel different, and she doesn't have that anxious feeling, that tightness she often experiences before her period. Rather she has been calm, much calmer than Kay, who bugs her about tests—as if a baby couldn't grow without a piece of paper and a lab result, without a doctor's permission, his little questions and probing fingers.

Holding her breath has reminded Claire of something, and, pleased with the memory, she bends her knees up and sits forward in the water. She lets her head and shoulders fall back into the bath until only her nose remains above the surface. She looks at the ceiling through the water. The room is quiet, but not silent. She can hear things. Her bum chafing against the porcelain. Water gurgling in the overflow drain. The soap settling on the bottom. The furnace in the basement two floors below. The breathing in her nose. Her pulse beating in her ears. She growls, making a sort of primeval grumble in her throat, and then stills her lungs. She imagines the blood moving through her veins, circulating through her tissues, all the veins and arteries, ligaments and lymph nodes. She wonders how many other people do this same thing, in their bath-tubs, their evenings, their lives. She is often overwhelmed thinking of all the people who are alive with her at this moment. Grandy making tea. Liz at the restaurant opening. Henley at sound check. Bob mixing paint. Salman Rushdie looking out the window ... Then a disturbing image of Patrick sitting in unzipped pants in front of the television flashes in and out of her mind so fast that a moment later she won't remember having it. Abruptly, Claire surfaces, takes a sputtery breath, tugs at the plug chain with her toe, and rises. She shakes her head briskly back and forth. Water runs off her pink and glowing skin back into the tub. She takes the towel from the radiator, rubs her hair, her face, her limbs and steps onto the bath-mat. With softly wrinkled hands, she spreads baby oil across her legs and buttocks and rubs it aggressively into her skin. A minute later, she has draped the towel over the radiator, turned off the bathroom light, and carried her clothes and book into her bedroom. Here she drops the clothes into a chair, lies across the bed with her book, and rests unbroken.

The Window

KAY HEARD THE PHONE ringing inside the apartment as she came up the stairs. She was hurrying the key into the deadbolt when the ringing stopped. The answering machine clicked, clicked again, then there was the sound of the dial tone.

She opened the door. Except for three green blinds that were outlined with yellow morning light, the room was dark. Kay pulled the chain on a floor lamp and glanced around. The apartment seemed as if it hadn't been occupied for a week or more. There were candy wrappers on the sofa, two or three Coke cans on a messy wooden desk, and torn pieces of paper strewn across the floor. Kay bent down to pick one up; it was beige vellum. On the other side was a charcoal drawing of an exaggerated male figure in a field beside some kind of animal. It looked like a bull or a horse. The way it was torn, Kay could only see its back legs.

"Will?" she called out, rising. "Hello? Anybody home?"

She went into the bedroom. She'd never been alone in this room before. There didn't seem to be anything unusual, though. The bedsheets were creased and twisted off one side of the bed, exposing a corner of the mattress. Beside the pillow was a quarter-full bottle of Evian water. Obviously dirty clothes—a T-shirt, a pair of jeans, a bathing suit—lay beside the clean, folded laundry at the foot of the bed.

On a short chest of drawers lay a much-squeezed tube of moisturizing cream. Kay, staring at it, wondered for a moment why it was there. Then, perversely, the details of the room shifted slightly, and took on an uncertain significance; Kay felt their unfamiliarity and the secret coincidence of her being alone in the room with them. With a burst of impatience, she went to the bed, picked up the Evian water, and emptied it into a sorry-looking fig tree that sat on the floor by the window. Then she went to the bathroom and threw the empty bottle in the white waste-paper basket.

The bathroom was tidy except for the water-stained sink and what looked to be week-old urine in the toilet bowl. Kay flushed the toilet but left inside the bowl was a ring of gummy yellow residue. She went to the window above the radiator and, her hands on either side, lifted it open. In between the storm and interior windows were two folded-up pages of loose-leaf. The pages were yellowed and rain-spotted. Kay swung open the wooden bar on the bottom of the storm window to let in some fresh air, then picked up and unfolded the loose-leaf. It was a letter dated October 13th, 1990, addressed care of Global Television, Toronto, and Kay read it as she wandered back to the living room.

Dear Will,

Hi how are you? It's me again. OK just in case you haven't got my first letter yet I'll start at the beginning. My name is Dale Glenn. I'm from Newberry, Vermont. I'm fourteen years old. That's just a little about me. I don't know a lot about you but in time I hope I will get to know more about you. I haven't heard from you yet, so I figured I'd try again.

So how are things now? I saw you in "Salamander Sunrise" and all my friends thought you were the funniest one (you were). You were excellent (take a bow). Were you nervous? How have you taken your success? Are you totally Canadian-based? I'd really like to get into a movie like that. Later on. I'd love to move up there to Ontario to try my luck in film. Do you speak French? I would like to make films similar to the U.S. but totally Canadian. I feel Canada should be able to make it on it's own without American support. Is it that way because it's the only way to get noticed?

I just feel proud to be Canadian-born. I love you're country. I often wonder about Canada, where it is, who is it with, what it is thinking about, is it thinking about me (Ha Ha!). Myself I think Canada must be very beautiful to live in. Do you go out partying much? Down here that's all you can do. If there's no party this place is dead.

What are your favorite groups? In my spare time I like to listen to music and read. How is Toronto? I went to Canada when I was ten, me and my mother's boyfriend and my friend's mother and hers. We had a good time there. The only problem was that it cost so much. We stayed at a part called Scarbourgh. It was nice there. I hope this year I'll get to go up again. There sure were a lot of tourists, the people I met from all around was unbelievable. You just can't imagine the people or maybe you can because you live there and have seen them. I don't really remember much of it though I have a rock in my room from Lake Ontario.

I sincerely hope you respond this time. Even a short letter saying "No time now Dale. Real letter later on" would be fine. It would let me know you've read my letter. Congratulations on your career! I'm sending a small photo of myself to give you the chance to see what I look like. I've copied both your movies and "The War of the Worlds" so I can see you on video whenever I want.

Please try and respond this time as soon as you can. I know I'm nobody special right now, but a response would mean a great deal to me. So please try! Take care of yourself and keep up the good work.

I am going on and on but I think I'll come to
an end. I'm really hoping that you will write me
back (Soon).

Yours Sincerely,

DALE GLENN
24 Wescott Road
Newberry, Vermont
29100

PS. Here is my picture. You should send me an
autographed picture of yourself. I would like to have one
of my own. We have an extra cot in the basement so any-
time you are in Vermont give me a call at 865-2324 or at
my father's 865-4582. And Smile! America is watching!

Kay refolded the letter and idly tapped it a few times against
her wrist. Then she dropped it on the desk and crossed the room
to snap up the blinds. Across Bloor Street she could see people
inside the blue windows of the Future Bakery. They were lining
up to buy coffee.

Kay poked her fingers into the soil of the potted plants
along the window sill. She shook her head and faced the room
again. The red light on the answering machine was flashing.
Kay went to it, pressed the play button, and continued to the
kitchen. As she waited for the tape to rewind and play, she ran
some water in the sink. Looking for a pitcher, Kay opened a
cupboard above the stove, only to be startled by a moth that flit-
tered out toward her and glanced off her cheek. In the next few
minutes, as she listened to the messages, Kay salvaged a glass
from the sink, used it to water the plants, gathered all the pieces
of vellum from the floor, then sat on the sofa and flipped
through the photographs of a *Honcho* magazine that she

retrieved from a toppling pile underneath the coffee table.

Beep: "Will. It's Bigley from mission control and we hope you're enjoying your posey little life. Where *are* you? You're on the guest list for Brian's annual Merry Widow party on Thursday. So call me."

Beep: "Will, it's Kay. It's Wednesday morning. So where were you? Correct me if I'm wrong, but isn't the director supposed to be at his own opening-night party? The stage manager said he watched the show with you, so where'd you go? I had to stand around all night talking to people like Davis Brewer who kept telling me what a big star he's going to be. I'm at work."

Beep: "Hi, Will. Pam calling. We seem to be playing phone tag. Sorry I didn't make it to the opening, but I didn't get through here until nine. Listen, could you give me a call at the office till six or at home after? It's about this script. We got a ten-page fax this morning and there's a few things I want to talk about. Thanks, Bye."

Beep: "Hello, Will. This is Mike. Mike Podowinski. Thanks a lot for the comps to the show, man. Best stuff we've seen in a while. Listen, we'll have to get together sometime. I have a show at the Theatre Centre in April, so maybe you can check it out. Bye-bye."

Beep: "Will, Pam again. You have a call-back on that astronaut movie. They want a video sent to LA, so which one do you want to send them, the long or the short? The short doesn't have your death scene from "War of the Worlds," but I think it's good enough. Call me, bye."

Beep: [*Dial tone.*]

Beep: "Would you please change that boring little *massage* on your machine? Are you there? Pick up the phone, please. You're suppose to be *home* now, Peter Pan. This is Kay calling. Kay Pritchard. I met you once in university. Why do I have a feeling you're listening to this message? It's Thursday. Call me.

I'm at work till seven. Or leave a message on my machine at home and I'll check it later."

Beep: "This is a message for William Westman. Mr. Westman, this is Frank O'Dacre's office returning your call. Mr. O'Dacre is away on discovery this week, but he will return next Monday. I suggest you call again at that time. If you need to speak to someone sooner than that, call 366-0044."

Beep: "Will? It's me. Are you there? Pick up the phone … I don't know where the hell you are. Anyway, it's official. We're losers. The show's cancelled. Friday's our last day."

Beep: [*Sounds of loud music.*] "Hello, Stephano? It's Marcello. Are you there …?"

Beep: [*Sounds of loud dance music.*]

Beep: *Dove stai, Stephano? Siamo aspettando per una ora.*

Beep: [*Dial tone.*]

Beep: "Listen, guys, I have to work tomorrow. It's too loud and it's too late so could you please turn it down?"

Beep: [*Dial tone.*]

Beep: "Hey, Will, turn-down-the-fucking-music!"

Beep: [*Dial tone.*]

After this message, the answering machine made three short beeps and shut off. Kay moved to the desk and finished looking through a photo-spread in the magazine. At the front of the desk were two empty Coke cans, the remote control for the television, a push-button phone and the Yellow Pages, lying open. Kay had just leaned forward to examine the pages when, as if it had been waiting for its cue, the telephone rang.

Kay reached for it, then, stealthily, pulled back her hand. After two rings, there was a short silence, another beep, two touch tones, then the tape began to rewind to the beginning. Kay brought the chair closer to the desk, put down the *Honcho* magazine, and, pretty sure who was on the other end of the phone, picked up the receiver.

"Will's Auto Body," she said.

There was a pause. "Kay?"

"Will, where are you?"

There was another pause. "I can't tell you."

"What do you mean you can't tell me—are you in jail?"

"Nobody knows where I am. Don't tell anyone you talked to me. It's just so horrible, Kay, you can't imagine."

"Oh, please. I can imagine a lot. Who's got you—Patty Hearst?"

"Not everything's a joke, Kay," Will said, his voice fatigued. "I'm serious."

"Oh, Will. What? What happened? Is it the reviews?"

"What are you doing there? What are you doing in my apartment?"

"I came to see if you were lying in a coma on your bathroom floor."

"How'd you get in? Did anyone see you?"

"I have a key, Will."

"Oh yeah," said Will. "Could you water the plants?"

"Well, that's the thing," said Kay, watching the tiny moth fly into the room from the kitchen and flutter across the grey television screen. "I think they've been kidnapped. Will, where've you been? Why weren't you at opening night? What the fuck is going on?"

"Oh my God, Kay," he said, sounding both tired and frantic. "How could I be so wrong?"

"Wrong about what?"

"I ripped up all his drawings."

"I noticed."

"He tried to sell my tuxedo."

"For coke?"

"How did you know?"

"It's not such a big secret."

There was a pause. "Well, anyway, his agent called to tell me that they're going to sue me and he evaluated Steph's drawings at twelve thousand dollars."

"Twelve thousand dollars!" Kay said, expressing her outrage to the empty room. "That's absurd."

"I know. He just used to sit around sketching them in bed. I didn't think they were that good. But he fucking sold everything, Kay. My tuxedo, my VCR, my clock radio. If anybody owes money it's him. And so now I'm going to need a lawyer. It's so dumb. It's so dumb. Why didn't you tell me I was in denial? I owe him twelve thousand dollars or I could go to jail. He was just so beautiful, Kay. How could he do this? I can't believe it. I can't believe I fell in love. I can't do that anymore …"

"Well, at least not with a cokehead, no matter how beautiful. You don't have twelve thousand dollars, do you?"

"No. Of course not. You don't think they're really worth that much, do you?"

Kay looked for the moth. She couldn't see it. "Offer him five," she said after a second. "You must have a couple grand and I have two, but you have to take care of this right away."

"Yeah, but is there a message on the machine from the lawyer?"

"You can't afford a lawyer, Will. Stephano's a cokehead. He just wants money. You just meet him with a letter and offer him five thousand and get him to sign it."

"I'm not seeing him again, Kay. I'm never *seeing* him. You have to do it."

"I'm not doing this. I'm not going—"

"Take Jordan with you. He'd love it. He loves that kind of undercover intrigue."

"Where is he? Where's Stephano?"

"How could I be so wrong about someone? We have to change the locks. I can't come home till we change the locks."

"Don't be so silly. You have to come home. This apartment's disgusting. You've got to clean this place up, Will. Where are you? Give me the number where you are."

"I know ... It was so beautiful until about three weeks ago. I mean I had to work, right? I had to get the show done. I couldn't entertain him all the time. I couldn't do everything for him, I couldn't. And he started bingeing and he couldn't stop. Oh my God, I'm so depressed. I'm so depressed. I thought I found this perfect, fabulous creature. How could I let myself think that? God, I'm such a sucker ..."

As Will continued his lament, Kay searched the desk for pen and paper. She found an uncapped red marker and, from the back of the desk, picked out a folded letter that lay flat on its middle third, either end in the air. On the back of this, she scribbled a faint but legible line. Checking the front to see if it was important, Kay saw that the letter was laserprinted and had an embossed letterhead. Quickly she read:

Casper Creek Productions
2121 Avenue of the Stars
Century City, California
90067

Mr. Will Weston
437 Brunswick Avenue
Toronto, Canada M5S 112

11 February 1992

Dear Will:

It was a pleasure to meet with you over lunch the other day in Toronto. I am sorry that we did not have time to get at some of the particular questions which you may have wished to raise, but both Miles and I feel that at least it was a very useful information exchange.

Pursuant to our letter of January 25, 1992, we showed the script to our friend at IAA, and he called us this morning to say that one of his clients, who asks to remain nameless, is very interested in the project pending rewrites. He is very interested in selling the idea from the Mork and Mindy/Moonstruck angle, and after meeting with him next week, we will be sending a detailed fax to your agent which will address the particular areas of the script we feel need revising.

Needless to say, if this actor is brought onside, we foresee no trouble at all raising funds for the picture and can realistically look at pre-production as early as Fall 1992 to shoot in the winter and spring.

We look forward to further meetings with you and hopefully with your collaborator, Ms. Pritchard, whom we wish a speedy recovery from her operation. Of course I must add, to avoid any hint of a misunderstanding, that this does not in any way oblige us to commit ourselves to the project, but Miles and I are both very impressed with the sense of energy and purpose you're bringing to the project, and very much look forward to working with you and Ms. Pritchard.

Please respond a.s.a.p. as we would like to know by the latest March 21 if you wish to pursue this matter.

Yours sincerely,
Fiona Venkman
for Miles Hoyland

Kay lurched forward in the chair. "Will!" she screamed. "What the fuck is this letter from Casper Venkman Productions?"

There was a short silence.

"Will? What fucking script is this? Why is my name mentioned?"

"You're a perfectionist, Kay," Will said. "And I was going to tell you—"

"Is it my script yes or no?"

"Look, they *love* it. They think it's great. They love the David Lynch small movie idea—"

"Is it mine?"

There was another silence. "Yes," Will said.

"Oh, you ... you fucking asshole! You sold them my script, you fucking asshole! Did you sign anything? Did you sign anything at all?"

"No," Will said. "At least, I don't—"

"Will fuck off. Fuck off. Did you or not?"

"No."

"You asshole. You fucking unforgivable asshole. This is the worst, this is the absolute worst you've ever done." Kay brought down her fist on the desk, causing one of the Coke cans to shiver off the edge and bounce onto the floor.

"Just calm down for one second, okay? For one—"

"And they think I collaborated with *you*? What did you tell them? How long have you been talking to these people?"

"Do you want to know how much money they're prepared to offer you?"

"Offer me? Aren't they offering it to us seeing that we wrote it together?"

"Kay, you're way too upset. Everything will be—"

"No, it won't. You blew it. You blew it this time, you fuck. You're a little fucking asshole, Will, you know that? And you better get that lawyer, pal. You're going to fucking need him."

Kay smashed down the phone and stood up, causing her

chair to tip over backward. She was halfway to the door when she heard it crash. She turned to look at the fallen chair. "What a fucking slob," she said, and gave the Coke can an almighty kick, sending it spinning across the floorboards toward the windows.

Air Canada
30,000 feet up

Monday March 16th

Dear Claire:
Just to go over what I said on the phone from the airport—on
my computer at my place is a file, C:\WP\MAYA\KEEP\
DRAFT.OLD. Copy this file onto one of the disks in the red
plastic container on the mantle, put the disk in a reinforced
envelope so that it doesn't bend, and then FedEx the entire
package to:

>   Kay Pritchard
>   c/o Casper Creek Productions
>   2121 Avenue of the Stars
>   Century City, CA
>   90067

But I need it ASAP because I realized in the taxi that I don't
have any copies of the first draft. My visa # is 4521 660 009 148
exp 02 93. Thanks heaps.

The guy beside me is driving me fucking crazy! He keeps clearing his throat and tilting his head and trying to read what I'm
writing. I guess his silver-embossed-cave-woman-complete
with-spear-and-flying-dragon book isn't holding his interest.

When he reads he mutters to himself, and I know he's just dying for me to ask him what he's reading. The flight attendant keeps giving me extra-special smiles, meaning the plane is full, I can't move you. And only four hours to go. But call me from my place if you have trouble with the disk. Toronto is three hours later then LA.

Sorry that I was such a harried cow and haven't spoken to you since all this stuff happened. I called after I came back from New York but Liz said you had just gone to a gallery opening.

So this is what happened. Last year Will meets a guy named Miles at a Festival of Festivals party and tells him he has a script. Miles tells Will to send it to Fiona, the director of acquisitions & development for an LA production company, Casper Creek. She likes it. She wants Miles to read it, but she can't ask him to read a 130-page screenplay so can Will, who said he was my writing partner, fax her a three-page synopsis? Will types one up and faxes it. "Look, Will," Fiona faxes back, "I've had very good response to the synopsis. I mean I think it's very strong material, some of the strongest we've seen in a while, and we're willing to make it a priority." Will being the unstoppably confident asshole that he is, tells me nothing and makes suggestions for changes and Miles and Fiona like them. They show the screenplay and the changes to this comedian they like named Junior Rideout, who's heavy into some other project. (I'd never heard of him but apparently he's done lots of television and minor film stuff. Do you remember a movie a couple summers ago called *Tokyo Giants* about baseball drop-outs who make it big in Japan? Junior's in that. He's the red-haired guy who gets into the sauna with the tiny Japanese men. At the meeting in New York, Fiona described Junior as "a Martin Short, Jim Carrey, Mike Myers type"—which I think is funny because they're all Canadian—"with boy-next-door looks"—meaning he's white, inoffensive and presentably cute—"and he's really level-headed"—meaning they can afford him and he's not going to upset Tipper Gore.)

So Junior wants more changes and Casper Creek writes Will a letter saying so and this was the letter I read that day at Will's place (who knows how long he would have strung me along if I hadn't). At this point a bunch of things happen all at once. For unspecified reasons (I think one of the other stars pulled out), Junior abruptly leaves his other project and tells Miles he's interested in theirs, namely mine. Then I call Casper Creek and explain that they're dealing with a lying weasel and that's when, because they know Junior won't be available for long, they bring me down to New York for a chat and to give me the pitch. Which for me sort of felt like this:

> MILES: We love the story, Kay, shy alien falls in love and defects to earth, it's great. And we love the Martian character, in fact—
>
> ME: He's not really a Martian, actually …
>
> MILES: —in fact we love *all* the Martian characters. But we see the script as being only about fifty to sixty per cent there right now.
>
> FIONA: Which for a first draft is excellent.
>
> ME: Actually he just tells Maya he comes from the sky. He's really—
>
> MILES: That's right, that's right. For a first draft it's excellent. But, as Junior and his people see it, and as Fiona and I see it, too, it needs to go a bit further. What we'd like to do is bring the basic premise out a bit more. It's just a matter of de-emphasizing the girl's family and concentrating more on the jeopardy aspects in the second and third acts.
>
> FIONA: Yeah, I think going further in that direction would be great. And we need to make it a little funnier too, you know.

ME: He's actually a homeless person that Maya meets
and—

MILES: That's right. We just need to lighten it a bit,
flesh out the plot line, kind of dimensionalize Marvin's
character, and then I think we'll be much closer to where
we want to be. Then we'll have a nice little romantic family comedy on our hands.

FIONA: How do you feel about that?

ME: Uh, what was that first thing?

And all through this I'm sitting there with little trickles of
sweat rolling down my armpits feeling like a fraud and wondering if it would look better if I picked up my pen and wrote
something on my new pad of paper. Then—FUCK! This weirdo
beside me is bugging me. He just rubbed his foot against my
ankle and he keeps pushing himself against me wanting me to
talk so I had to cross my legs and face the other way and now
he's radiating nerdy hate-vibe at me—then we all went out to
dinner and they gave me Junior's demo reel and copies of his
standup. Miles, the guy with the cash (you can just tell) I have
my few doubts about, as Mom would say, but Fiona I think I'll
like a lot. They were both very charming and smart and if I
hadn't known that most producers screw-and-schmooze for a
living, I'd have been quite dazzled. As a matter of fact, they
were so schmoozy, I feel quite confident that they know what
they're doing. They offered me about 15% more than the going
rate, and, rather than have them assign some hack writer to do
re-writes, they decided I'm hack writer enough to do it, though
I will be working with at least one other screenwriter whom I
meet tomorrow, when we'll be "chunking down the script into
manageable areas."

Selling it is the right decision. Of course I was totally bewil-
dered when I found out, but after talking to everybody, Angela,

Peggy, Peggy's agent, I realized that it's a very, very lucky break and I would be colossally foolish not to take advantage of it. I know for a fact that it's going to be drastically changed (I think the storm scene's gone already), but I should get a solo screenwriting credit and it won't be the last project I'll ever work on. To tell the truth, to make it on my own was seeming pretty impossible. First, I hadn't worked the script into what I wanted yet—part of the reason why I got so angry with Will—and second I was realizing that low-budget movies either cost no money (like $50,000) or giant money (a million), and I was caught in between.

New York was great. I walked around for a couple hours after the meeting, trying to remember what I was worried about in Toronto. I stayed at The Chelsea, not only the same hotel but the same floor where Sid killed Nancy. At night you could hear the radiator banging. I woke up at four in the morning and couldn't sleep, listening to the noise. "It's Nancy," I thought, lying there. "It's Nancy still trying to get some attention." Spooky. Imagine that we should have idolized them, and that all those boys were convinced that Sid stood for purity.

The woman in the window seat just got up to go to the washroom and the asshole wouldn't budge, he just pushed his table tray up and made her squish her bum past his face. What a sorry-assed science fiction dweeb. Now I'm really hating him.

Thanks for agreeing to send me that stuff, Claire. I'll talk to you soon. They're handing out the headphones now for the movie. Okay, so here I go making some fucking schmoozy Hollywood product.

Pray for me,
Kay

(I hope Tasha has come out of her room by the time you get this.)

♦

Century Plaza Hotel
2025 Avenue of the Stars
Los Angeles, CA
90067

March 18th

Dear Grandy:
What a lovely letter! It arrived the morning I left. And you don't have to worry—I'm driving everywhere and the hotel has great security. Yes, they have me on a pretty tough schedule here and yes, I am on the look-out for Elizabeth Taylor. Esther Williams, however, may be a little harder to find. The fellows I'm working with have promised to take me to a big Hollywood party, so I'll see what I can do. What about Bob Hope? Is he any good to you? Actually, I told them we're not so easily impressed. I told them we knew Louis B. Mayer when he was dealing scrap metal in Saint John. They didn't seem to get the joke, though. Yes, Mom had told me about Mr. Jacobson's store going out of business. I guess I'm a little surprised it didn't happen earlier. Was it the last one? And that was a chain, wasn't it, all through the Maritimes? Poor old Highfield Square. I still remember Claire and I comparing new bathing suits in Jacobson's parking lot—our first bikinis, hers flourescent orange, mine pink.

So I'm going to test the waters down here for a while, then I think I'll take a few weeks off and make some decisions. I'd like to come and finally visit down there—I mean it this time!—if it's all right with you. Are you still planning to go to the cottage this summer? If you tell me your dates early enough, maybe I can drive you down.

I am sorry to hear about your cold. I know you're not crazy about doctors, but you don't want to fool around, even with a cough. But that was a wonderful letter. I especially enjoyed hearing about your days in Montreal before Ganpy. I think we should sit you down in front of a video camera and get you to tell all those stories. It would be great to have the family history assembled somewhere.

Hope the spring comes early and stays late,

Love,
Kay

♦

Century Plaza Hotel
2025 Avenue of the Stars
Century City, CA
90067

March 19th

Dear Will:
Saw you in my dream last night. I introduced you to Miles as Harold Hollier. Sorry.

I haven't seen LA yet. These first few days have gone by in a blur. Every day I get up, shower, wait for my writing partner

Felix to pick me up and take me down to the Casper Creek offices where we talk about the script from ten till seven and he says things like, "Okay, now is the Marvin character like a humanoid on his planet, or are his people just like a bad special effect?" Or he says, "Movies don't go that long without dialogue, Kay." And I say, "Sure they do." And he says "Can't make a movie without dialogue, Kay." And I laugh, thinking he's joking but he's not. Or he says, "What are you trying to do in this storm scene?" And I say, "What do you mean?" And he says, "It's too heavy. It's like some gothic-chick Jane Eyre rainstorm. I'm afraid we're going to have to cut this little homage to Tarkovsky." (Never mind that it's what made me want to write the movie in the first place). Then after lunch Felix says, "I don't know if Maya's the type of person who would do this." And I say, "Sure she is." And he says, "No. I don't see her like that at all." And then we meet with Miles, and he says things like, "There are too many small scenes that don't go anywhere," or "There's still some logic problems you haven't addressed yet," or "What about the jeopardy in the third act?" (They're very keen on this jeopardy stuff.) Then we adjourn to a restaurant, and after dinner, I leave them all to their little clandestine conversations about release dates and Q-ratings and I take a taxi home where I collapse, and we do it all over again the next day. Basically we have to fucking replot the whole second half of the movie. The whole focus of the film has been warped over to Marvin now. All my little life-things and ambiguities are quickly and surely being tossed out. So it's becoming a new movie, and as Felix reminds me every morning, it *has* to become a new movie because "who the hell's going to pay six bucks to see a movie about a chick that nothing happens to? Sally Field gets a cramp? Forget it." I'll send you some of the rewrites to show you how they're killing me.

Felix is about thirty-five, getting a belly and generally seems to babysit me. He and Junior, whom I finally met and liked, have been writing together for the last ten years or so. There used to be a third musketeer, Eddie, who's apparently really funny but has a little problem with being a junkie and who's the bane of Felix's existence. So when I met Eddie (he dropped by the office this morning) I expected him to be the comedy-asshole who's always on but he turns out to be this tall guy who's very quiet and who tells me within five minutes of having met me that I'm the only person in LA he trusts. Hello?... But you mention this guy Eddie's name and bingo-bango Felix goes nuts and starts spitting when he talks. Felix was freaked all day today after Eddie left because Eddie is invited to the party tomorrow at Zitzerman's, which I thought was another restaurant, but which turns out to be another producer.

Junior reminds me of you a bit. He's by far one of the most competent people I've met and he knows his talents and his limits very well. When we pitch him new ideas he sits very still with his eyes closed. He never says what he doesn't like, but once in a while he jumps up and starts improvising and I start laughing really, really hard and can't stop and everyone feels embarrassed for me. He's so quiet and serious that when he gets light and enthusiastic, I'm always surprised. I'm just thrilled he isn't one of those one-upping love-me need-me schizo pricks. I think he's having an affair with Mickey, his five-hundred-dollar-a-week personal assistant, who just got a Ph.D. in linguistics from Princeton and who wears big hoop earrings (yup, it's true) and, of course, the ubiquitous baseball cap. But I have her to thank, evidently, because according to Eddie, Junior wanted a script Mickey liked and it was her suggestion that they work with the original writer. And now that Junior's into it, people are ludicrously confident and say things like, "It's going to be really big, Kay. People are going to fucking love this picture. It's got everything." Okay ... Hello.

Can you do a big favour for me? Claire was supposed to send me a disk with the script on it but I don't need it now because I photocopied the draft they had down here (I won't need it anyway). So can you tell her to forget about sending it? I've tried to call her a hundred times but her phone's been disconnected so could you also ask her to call me collect. She lives at 468 Palmerston. And tell her to call Mom. Tell me she isn't pregnant. Just tell her to call me collect anyway.

Sorry I got so mad the day I left but if you were going to keep talking about the script like it was yours I was going to have to hit you. And sorry that you're so poor. But you'll be rich soon, right? The astronaut movie will start paying you immediately. Then you'll be able to move back home, pay everyone off, and still have money left over to buy me a present.

Love ya,
Kay

P.S. You know when I left you said that the worst thing that could happen was the script is rejected, the company goes bankrupt, can't pay me and I never get a job again? I've been thinking about that. I think the worst thing that could happen is that the script is rejected, the company goes bankrupt and can't pay me, and the CBC gives me my own show.

Hey, did you ever write that kid whose fan letter I found in your bathroom window? Write him. Write me, too, eh? I feel cut off. I feel cut off from me roots, b'y.

Hi Kay,

Nothing works out. That's all I can say. Nothing ever works out. I just got off the phone with Agent Pam about the astronaut movie. After screaming at her for three weeks to finalize my contract, she finally tells me that I've been written out. Due to scheduling problems, constant rewriting was required in order to keep shooting. "What a shame," Pam says. "They really liked you. And the money they were talking about was quite good. Apparently it was quite a nice part. What a shame. And you know absolutely everything else this summer's been cast. It's very slow now. Dead." (But they really did like me, right?) What's worse is that Michael Podowinski's part is still in—which is a shame BECAUSE HE CAN'T ACT! He's got Terminal Actor Voice and he's the same in everything. But no big deal. That movie was going to save my year, that's all. I already said no to Stratford. I could've been fucking Benedict and Mercutio again. And I turned down the Dieppe movie too. Waaa. I had this nice little fantasy where I was going to have my birthday on set and Morgan McCarthy and everybody would stop shooting because they had a big cake for me ... Nothing works out, Kay. That's all I can say.

Last year Nelvana couldn't get enough of me for voice-overs. On "Rupert the Bear" alone I did a dragon, an uncle and a whole family of horses. Pam called them this morning, I can't even get a fucking frog now. The only thing she found is an audition for a Xerox industrial on how to clean photocopiers. My life is a joke—except I'm still in it! I'm not happening. The future's not happening, and the days are going by and they're nothing. And everywhere you go it's the high season. You can't ride your bike without running into a film crew. There are thirty major productions shooting here this summer and I'm not in any of them.

So while you're lounging by the pool waiting for your escort to take you to the Dorothy Chandler Pavillion (I'm very jealous but I'm trying not to be—tell me what happens at that Zitzerman party, I'm dying to get the scoop, are these Felix-Eddie people Fuck or Die or what?) while you're there and Stephano is asleep in my bed, I'm still hiding out here at Dean's in a squishy little room, waiting to get my apartment back and sort of wallowing in this shitty little fucked-up existence where I don't have any money and have to beg people for work. Dean's is like a way station for lost homosexuals at the moment. (People like Dean have bottomless cups of forgiveness and tolerance, while I only seem to have a tart little espresso.) Besides me and Dean's young man, there's a friend of Dean's—Casey MacKinnon from Cape Breton—who looks like a muppet. He was the star of last summer's Stephenville Festival, now he's up here trying to be an actor. I sent him off to get his resume laser printed and to check the bulletin board at Equity Showcase. Personally I don't care if I direct another play again. Only your friends come, you're just taking money from your friends, it's a fucking pyramid scheme. We won't even discuss reviews. I'll probably never get another grant. Did I mention that nothing works out?

Midnight Saturday. Can't sleep. Casey and I just got back from working on a Sleeping Dogs video that Jordan got us. (Jordan's nice. He bugs me, but he's on the nice side of he bugs me.) We shot it in the warehouse where I used to do War of the Worlds. Except instead of doing a thirty-minute scene for $600, I worked with a grip for 16 hours for $100. We worked with that guy Dan you went to film school with. (That's $25,000 worth of André Bazin's auteur theory pulling plywood off that half-ton!) He's been working in Vancouver on a TV series where, he didn't mind telling me, he made a lot of money and lived with Walker Young who's a junkie now. Remember him? That sleeping dog Henley is some awfully cute boy. Thought I'd see Claire there but didn't. Dropped by her pad twice but no one home.

In two weeks I'm going to be thirty years old, Kay. Thirty. Closer to forty than I am to 18. There must be some mistake. I wish I'd started trying to get things done sooner. I feel like one of those out-of-work guys in the newspaper. I just want to work. Is that really so awful? That's all I've ever really wanted to do. I don't want to be an Edith Piaf song. I'm never going to own a car. I'm never going to get to travel. I'm never going to live in Europe. No one's ever going to love me again.

love Harold

P.S. Pam's sending my audition tape to you so could you please give it to Fiona. I know we could send it directly to her, but it'll be better if it comes from you. You don't have to suck her bean or anything. Just ask her to look at it, okay, please.

W

♦

Century Plaza Hotel
2025 Avenue of the Stars
Century City, CA
90067

Oscar Night

Dear Will:
Thanks for your letter. I got it today and in a perverse way it cheered me up. Any word from Claire? I still haven't heard from her. I'm a little worried. That's horrible about the astronaut

movie. But what ever happened to Super-Will, the guy who got the grant, the guy who thought New York was no big deal, the guy whose play was going to kick butt while the rest of us were looking around for our lives?

And how am I? Thirty thousand on the first day of shooting, thirty thousand on the first day of shooting ... That's my mantra. That's what's getting me through this. It's 4 o'clock. Junior's having a big Oscar party at his house. I don't really feel like going, but I have to. Eddie's going to pick me up after the pre-show, where they show all the people lining up and going in and screaming and waving at Kim Basinger. I feel like sooking and watching them alone in my hotel room with a big bag of barbecue chips. Felix and I had a fight about the script this morning. I'm exhausted. I've been so stressed out about work. Last night I tried to call you at Dean's, but I couldn't remember his number offhand, and then I remembered that day at The Senator when you told me he'd lost his address book. And I told you how when we were kids Claire thought if I tried really hard I could remember her memory for her. So I thought it would be great if Marvin could remember other people's memories and he would go on a quest in search of Maya's mother's memory. Felix, who's paranoid that he's going to be replaced because we haven't produced enough, said the idea sucks. I hate it when he doesn't think exactly like I do. I'm starting to play games where I don't say what I really want in the hopes that I can manipulate him into thinking what I want later, which generally makes me feel more professional. The script is so totally fucked, Will. We're ruining in two weeks what took two years. Of course I knew all about be-prepared-to-kill-your-baby stuff, but I didn't think the movie would become *Police Academy 42*. Marvin is now a total alien, and there is a whole other storyline about him and the police, and people from his home planet who come to look for him ... All the silent parts—Maya walking home in the snowstorm, Marvin's sunrise scene—all of them, gone. The worst thing is that they're trying to turn Maya into "the kooky girlfriend." Just what movies need, right, another flakey dum-dum female character. I think Felix is picturing Geena Davis or someone. This morning in the middle of the argument he stops dead, and says, "Wow, you ever think about acting, Kay?"

"Why?"

"You see *Bringing Up Baby*?"

"Yeah. Why?"

"In that skirt you look exactly like Katharine Hepburn. I didn't know you had legs like that. You mean you never thought about acting?"

I say nothing.

"What? What did I say? Boy, I can never say the right thing around you, can I?"

Thirty thousand on the first day of shooting, thirty thousand on the first day of shooting ...

But you want to know about Zitzerman's party. It was very crowded, very white wine sushi gossip mineral water who's that aren't those and isn't that more sushi. But the house, Will, you should have seen this house! Zitzerman made $8.8 million producing *Tokyo Giants* so he bought this art-deco mansion that overlooks the valley. He had an artist who lives out in the desert put in this enormous stained-glass window that looks like Montreal civic art circa 1967. He also put a pond in the backyard, which according to Eddie has to be re-done every year because by February it's a mud puddle. I arrived starving (bad idea) and stood guard over the hors d'oeuvres for about an hour. One guy came up to me, Ollie Cantor. Have you heard of him? I had no idea who he was. To me he was just the guy hogging the tempura. In fact he seemed kind of lost so I told him to look me up if he ever came to Toronto. Then I gave him my card and I told him *maybe I could do something for him.* "So who is he?" I ask Eddie later.

"What do you mean, that's Ollie Cantor."

"Yeah ...?"

"He just signed a three-picture deal with Touchstone. He's on Arsenio all the time. I thought you knew him." Swell. My God, we got drunk. I'm sure I made a great impression on everybody. I've been having little I-can't-believe-I-said-that flashbacks all day. This other guy came up and gave me his resume, "Hi I'm Barry Whoever and last year I worked on blah blah blah ..." I couldn't believe it. I thought it was a joke. Who talks like that? You can't be a human being talking like that.

"Who, Barry Kopeck?" Eddie said. "He's not a human being. He's a nobody. Don't even talk to that guy. He's even smaller than we are. He's not even a nobody, he's a nothing."

Makes me wonder what they said about me when I went back for more sushi. Your skirt was a big hit, by the way; everybody in LA wears the same floral print dress.

LA. I don't know. I just don't know if I make a very good LA person. I don't know if anyone does. It's very strange to think that some of the most talented people in the world come here to get rich. Everyone's beautiful—even 75 yr old women are beautiful—and so many women have gravity-defying breasts that wherever I go I feel like I'm walking into a commercial for beer or power tools. When I first got here, I was kind of surprised at how normal and friendly people were, and then slowly I began to realize they weren't. They're not exactly cocksucking vampires either, but this place is so snakes and ladders that it fucks you up if you don't have anything else to refer to. Eddie's been here eight years, and he hasn't met anyone who isn't in the business. And it's very transient. You work with people for three months, they're your best friends, then the show ends and you

never see them again. Or if you do, you're probably more interested in impressing each other than hanging out. This place is
full of fear, pure and complicated. Still, there's a beautiful,
ephemeral quality about all of it that's very seductive. And
stressful. No one feels safe about their jobs is why. No one feels
safe about anything.

And you, you're working on rock videos with people who know
Walker Young. I had this great idea for a video, actually. It's a
field, and there's a guy in a leather jacket walking around, and
there's some slow-motion shots of a model in bare feet and a
depression-era dress with some of her buttons undone. Then you
cross-cut some B&W footage of a wrinkled old man on a high-
way, preferably a native Indian or a wise old black man, and
then, here's the outrageous part, you have the guy in the leather
jacket ... start playing a guitar!

I decided a while ago that there are four general phases for
women. First you go out with really cute but always terminally
immature cool boys. You go out with them till you're about 24
and then you realize you can't save them and that you better get
out while you can. Then you go out with an older man with a
flat stomach who eventually screws you over to go out with
another twenty-four year old. Then you find a decent guy who
treats you well and you move to Italy, or to suburbia somewhere.
And then when you're forty, you have an affair with a woman
because your husband is having an affair with a twenty-four year
old. Now that I think about it, there are probably more phases,
but I'm too tired to think of them. I think they all end up with
the guy and a twenty-four year old anyway.

Walker Young. We were the clever kids in first-year English.
He was the loner, though, where I was always the joiner. I think
he liked me for my quickness, but he was part sympathetic and

part aloof and even when we went out I could sense that he regarded me with contempt. He quit halfway through second year and hung around York for a while before moving downtown to live in the ghetto of cool people. Fuck, I know the whole routine. Downtown groovers. Pony-tails, black jeans, black leather jackets, maybe a motorcycle—and a chick. That's what you do in the ghetto. You act like a chick. You live for a man. Preferably one with talent. Painter, musician, sculptor, whatever. He's probably in a band or he has friends in a band. You encourage him. No one understands him. You work. He sleeps. You pay the rent. He buys the hash. You're probably a waitress. You drink a lot of beer at night and smoke some hash after your shift. You try to convince him to go back to school. You think about going back to school yourself and you read a lot of useless highly theoretical books by French feminists, in case anyone asks. And then it gets to be five years later and you're still there. Watching all his friends slide out of the bottom of life, wondering how it happened.

Of these guys, there are: (1) guys who get over it (2) guys who don't know how to get over it but constantly reassure you that their life is okay and (3) guys who really have talent. (Those guys go on to become Eric Fischl or David Byrne or Oscar Peterson—those guys don't need saving.) At any time the number 2s can become number 1s or 3s, but they don't really have to because every three years a new roster of young women will be waiting to buy into their authenticity.

Jordan kept a nice balance by getting and keeping a record job. But sure, until I got the Nightcap job, I felt a little like his accessory. There is no end to the men who want a smart-talking tart on their arm to make them feel smart, hip and unhappy. But Jordan will be fine because basically he's a good guy, and though you may think differently, he doesn't need to make people think that he's more than he is.

The whole bit with cool boys is that they want to have more mystique than they have. They're funny and smart and they have a great take on things—but more often than not they're losers. It's the same old story. Smart talented losers. My early twenties were littered with cool boys in leather jackets who made fun of everything. That's all I went out with. But those guys had no goals. They never *tried* anything, you know, but boy, did they make fun of those who tried and fucked up. And people who were successful were immediately derided and dismissed because they had sold out or because they hadn't suffered enough and therefore didn't have an edge. Cool boys don't feel they deserve success so no one else does either. All my boyfriends, they were torn between being cool and having a future. Guess which one they chose? And I'm a corporate whore because I finally decided at the age of 25 that I was sick of instability and laundromats and that I was going to take my life seriously? I mean, when you're young, it's kind of exciting to have negative feelings about things, but this is like ten years later, guys. You don't have to argue about pop music anymore. You don't have to have an opinion about Psychic TV or Billy Idol. You don't have to worry about *Heavy Metal* magazine. It's true. I went out with guys who used to jerk off to cartoons ...

And Walker, even though he fucked around a lot of people and could be an obnoxious abusive bastard, to hear that he's a junkie now in Vancouver isn't so much of a relief somehow. God, it's pretty terrible to think that being in a punk band in high school was the high point of his life. If this film ever comes out, Walker will say it's the greatest thing when he sees me, but when I'm gone he'll have to say I sold out—which I suppose I have—and he'll dismiss it. He dismisses everything. He perfected the art of taking things too seriously and not seriously enough at the same time. Sirens, that's what cool boys are.

Of course that's just my opinion. They could still prove me wrong.

I've had crazy insomnia since arriving here. I think the plane trip threw me off. I'm really tired. And I smell like a monkey.

Kay

♦

30 Mar 1992
Dean's (still)

Kay,

Bigley's having everyone over to watch the Oscars but I'm not into it. I'm so tired of myself. The last few weeks I've been re-thinking my life as in, What am I doing, what do I want to do, why do I owe so much money, what if this is the most successful I'll ever be, what do I have to do to get myself where I want to go, why was I so stupid as to have chosen to be an actor and shouldn't I get a proper job etc etc etc. We all want to be better, though, don't we? We all want to be stars. Except Dean. Dean has the courage not to be a star. Dean has the courage to be a homeowner. Dean owns his own house. I'm renting an apartment I don't even live in. I've got bad karma, Kay. I'm having bad karma month. I'm fucking terrified I've built up too much bad karma. I wish I got thirty thousand dollars on the first day of shooting.

God, I just tuned in to the Oscars. I can't believe those dancers. Every year it looks more and more like Carol Burnett.

Casey MacKinnon crashed an understudy audition for the touring show of Joseph and the Technicolor etc and got it. He's going on tour for a year for a thousand dollars a week … My friends' lives are either ridiculously successful or on the verge of tragedy. Or both. Like mine.

Like Stephano's. Yes, well. The day I wrote that letter to you I went to meet Stephano at Bar Italia to give him his cheque, and you would have liked me, I was so good. The last time we talked it was a bitchfest scene from hell. I called him and told him to get his shit out of my apartment. He screamed, I shouted, he swore, I swore, he hung up, I hung up. Then I called him back and said he could stay till April 1st, which is when his studio sublet in New York is over. But what could I say anyway? I didn't have the rent. I've got fuck all. He has my rent. He's got all my fucking money (and yours and Rodney's). I told him he should do something about that habit of his. What's the last thing he says to me? "We are not all as careful as you, Will. We cannot all be like you." His little friends playing boccetta, smiling at me as I walk away. There's a lesson in there somewhere, right? If he ever turns into a star, I'm going to tape those drawings back together and sell them for a fucking fortune.

On Saturday, after working all day on another video, I worked as a banquet waiter with Bigley at L'Hotel, the hotel next to the convention centre. We served 245 pharmaceutical salesmen and their spouses. I'm setting tables with my partner, Maria, wine glass, three forks, two knives, dessert spoon, dessert fork, teaspoon, coffee cup, saucer, bread and butter plate and knife ("You do the butter and cream, I'll do the waters. How many tables we got? Six tables of eight? Is the bread down? Let's hurry so we can go down for break.") Who walks in but your Moncton friend, that Chris McGuire guy. He stared at me all night trying to figure out how he knew me. After dinner the remaining husbands got very drunk and rowdy. "Hey little fucker," one says, "Where you going?" "Hey, big fucker, no where." And all their wives, it's probably one of the few times

*

they put on party dresses and go out, here they were ordering their white wine spritzers and going back to their tables while their sweaty husbands, now without ties and jackets, shirts undone, are on the dance floor shouting Play some Stones! Play some Stones! Rock and Roll! And the DJ puts on Hot Hot Hot and everybody starts bunny hopping across the dance floor, falling and laughing like it's the best night of their life. And I'm standing anonymously against the wall, waiting for them to go so Maria and I can clean up, thinking "Oh my God, this is depressing. This is the most depressing place in all of Canadian theatre."

I just realized I didn't thank you for returning my earring. Do you remember that night you dressed up in your little ska outfit and we went to stand in line in the stairwell of the VooDoo Club to see Mink De Ville (I still don't know why we went to see him) and that girl that stood across from us with grey make-up all over her face looking so cool? God that was exciting. It was so early eighties, and I know in ten years I'll think, God, fucking Stephano, fucking astronaut movie, fucking Joseph and his fucking Technicolor Dreamcoat and Kay and Junior Rideout … So people will look back on us and say, "It's that whole 1990s thing." Every ten years we get to reorganize the last decade. It's all a very Sesame Street kind of reasoning, isn't it?

U deserve something, Kay. I don't know. A guy. A house. A horse. What is it?

Will

◆

[*Crammed on the back of a postcard of Los Angeles with the words "Man dig those crazy Los Angeles freeways" stretched across the sky in red ink.*]

Can I ask you a question? Are you happy with your first 30 years? Are you doing now what you expected you'd be doing? What do you want to do in the next ten years? When do you think you were at your cutest? Have you considered using wrinkle cream? What person were you the meanest to? Have you had a happy sex life? Do you think the truth is good for people? Do you tell lies to help yourself? Do you remember what you were like as a kid? What do you want to do tomorrow? Why do you think we're so obsessed with achievement? Do you still look for sex? Is it lonely looking for sex? Have you considered using wrinkle cream? Will you ever sleep with a woman again? Are you a disciplined person? Do you want to be a parent? Are you still enamoured of genius art boys? Is Stephano watering your plants? How much money do you think you can be comfortable on? Where do you think prejudice comes from? How are you prejudiced? Do you think people can only be good at one thing? What have you done that you wish you did better? What's the worst thing you've done in your life? What are you doing tonight? Have you considered using wrinkle cream? How's your Mom? Do you still see your family? Are you happy with your body? Do you have the body you've always wanted? Does anyone else want it? Have you ever bought Preparation H? Have you considered using wrinkle cream? Do you miss me? Do I love you? Happy Birthday William Osborne Weston who is thirty years old in the year 1992, love K.

◆

[*On the back of a picture post card of a smoggy Los Angeles sunset with the words "All's well that ends well—Los Angeles" stretched across the sky in red ink.*]

Dr. J. Kovacs 170 Bloor W. Tor. CANADA. Lost job, finished screenplay, had screenplay stolen, found screenplay, sold screenplay, came here to rewrite screenplay, got breast implants, sold breast implants, had breast implants stolen. If movie is made, plan to swear off all worldly goods and retire a nun in Tibet (if I can find her). Best, Kay

♦

Eddie:
I believe this is yours. I was going to do you the honour of returning it in person but I think this is where I get off.

This morning after I'd convinced Felix that I'd simply taken home another Latino boy from the hotel staff (it wasn't easy explaining missing the Oscars—it's like missing fucking Christmas with your mother) Miles, whom I've decided is the sound of fingernails on a blackboard made into a person, called and told me that (1) Junior loves the other-people's-memory idea now and (2) Miles thinks I've done a great job but "what the project really needs now is another perspective," and I realize that you are that other perspective and that you probably knew all along. Miles is smart. I always said he was smart.

So you've got Maya now. Please take care of her and resist the temptation to turn her into a shell-shocked cat. Don't let them turn her into a nothing. Remember why you liked her in the first place. Or ask Mickey, if you forget.

So best of luck and I hope you get out of here sometime soon. Eight years is too long, even if the rest of the world is slowly coming to you. In case you ever come looking for me in New Brunswick, I think I should mention that it's not really a suburb of Toronto, it's somewhere north of Maine, and I don't live there anymore. Mississauga is a suburb of Toronto, too, but I don't live there either.

And sorry, but you're wrong. I say now as I said then, Annette Bening had the best dress.

So now I need another idea.

Kisses,
Kay

♦

INT. MAYA'S MOTHER'S HOUSE—DAY

T I N A, Maya's sister, stands in the hallway holding her six-year-old S O N. Together they look at the track of wet footprints that leads up the stairs.

> SON
> Where's Aunt Maya going, Mom?

> TINA
> Shhh, honey.

> SON
> Isn't Grandma sleeping?

> TINA
> Shh.

Maya walks into her mother's bedroom. She is still carrying the toy horn and her blue coat is covered in snow. Her mother, MRS. MAGDENKO, is asleep.

O.S. floor creaking.

CU MOTHER sleeping.

> MAYA
> (O.S.)
Mama …

> MOTHER
> (WAKING)
Huh? Maya? Where is he? Where's what's-his-name?

> MAYA
> (A BEAT)
He went home.

> MOTHER
What do you mean home? He's homeless.

> MAYA
I mean he went back.

Maya sits on the edge of her mother's bed and smiles. Her mother sits up and takes her hand. She looks at Maya a moment more before beginning to cry.

EXT. STREET—DAY

MARVIN has chased the poodle into a marching band. In the b.g., an unmarked police car follows behind him.

> MARVIN
> (LAST DITCH)
> Mr. Brian ... Mr. Brian ...

COP #1 leans out of window with his best Sgt. Bunz.

> COP #1
> Hey, you, Tarzan. That's far enough.

Marvin reacts to the voice by fainting.

EXT. POLICE STATION—DAY

Establishing shot of police station. A patrol car passes in front of camera, wiping frame, as we hear:

> COP #1
> (O.S.)
> When was the last time you saw Maya Magdenko?

INT. POLICE STATION—DAY

Marvin is sitting down at a table being questioned by the two cops. He looks exhausted.

> COP #1
> (CONT'D)
Marvin, we don't want you to get in any more trouble. All we want to know is where Maya Magdenko is, that's all.

Marvin looks from one cop to the other.

CU COP #2

SOUNDTRACK: Marvin's MEMORY MUSIC but erratic tempo.

CU MARVIN remembering.

> MARVIN
> (CONFUSED)
Cup of flour. Half a cup of white sugar. Half a cup a goddam homeless guy. We're wasting our time on some homeless guy.

> COP #2
> (SURPRISED)
What'd you say?

Marvin turns from Cop #2 and sees WANTED MAN PHOTOGRAPH on wall.

CU WANTED MAN PHOTOGRAPH.
We recognize him as the man who had been in the restaurant with Maya.

SOUNDTRACK: Marvin's MEMORY MUSIC very
erratic tempo.

ECU MARVIN remembering.

FADE OUT

END ACT THREE

Liz's Opinion

CLAIRE CLIMBS UP THE STEPS of the Bathurst subway station. She has been up all night and in the same clothes for the last three days: olive-green thermal undershirt, jeans without underwear, cowboy boots and work socks. It's eight o'clock on Friday morning and the subway stairs are busy with school children, teenagers, men and women on their way to work ...

Claire watches a crowd of people hurry past her to catch the train she's just left. She returned Bob's painting yesterday and ended up staying for dinner, and then overnight. But instead of sleeping together, they stayed up talking, arguing, drinking red wine, and crying till five in the morning when they declared themselves friends and went out for breakfast. Claire drank five cups of coffee and now, with the sun rising and a new day starting, she feels at once wakeful and sluggish. Standing in the subway, she felt herself pass over a sort of fatigue threshold and, though she knows she has missed a lot of sleep, she thinks of getting Tasha out of bed to come out for more coffee. For Claire's day is very simple. She has to go to the university to double-check the time and place of her two exams, deposit a rent cheque in Liz's account, then come back and have a nap. She can't remember if Tasha needs money for her rent. She will ask her when she gets home. She remembers now, too, that Patrick has his thesis defence today. If it is successful, he wants people to take him out for drinks and get him drunk, like at Oxford.

Coming up to the apartment, Claire is feeling quietly confident, pleased that she has only the exams to worry about, when she notices that the door is open. The cat suddenly overtakes her on the stairs and scrambles into the hallway. Once inside, Claire has trouble seeing in the dim half-light, her eyes not yet adjusted, but she hears a tapping noise and, noticing that the bathroom door is closed, follows this noise to the living room. Liz sits alone in the love seat, wearing her leather jacket. She is staring at a grey sticky stain on the floor and flicking her thumb against the upholstery; it makes a little twang. In her other hand she holds a new phone bill.

"How was the conference?" Claire says, sitting side-saddle on the arm of the sofa and watching the cat roll over on the floor. "You just get back?"

Liz doesn't move. She stops twanging her thumb. "I thought you guys were going to get the phone reconnected while I was away," she says.

Claire puts some loose hair behind her ear. She knows she has been irresponsible about money. She owes money to Bob, to her sister, to her grandmother, even to Patrick. In fact she has lived the last month on ninety dollars, eating rice and lentil soup. Her plan was to go tree-planting with Bob in May, but now that she and Bob are over, she knows she won't go, though she is still vaguely counting on the money. "I was kind of enjoying not being terrorized by the phone," she says.

Liz glares at Claire. "You know how much money we owe, Claire?"

"For the phone?"

"For the phone. For the rent. For gas. For hydro." Liz rubs at the stain with the heel of her boot. "Did you know that Tasha doesn't have her rent?"

"What?"

"She said she told you before I left."

"She talked to you?" Claire slides down onto the sofa. As she sits up straight, arching her back, she is aware again of the right. Tasha has been a problem. She sleeps all day, doesn't get dressed, doesn't go out, doesn't shower, only leaves her bedroom when no one else is home, and then only to watch television. Claire worries that the gallery opening made everything worse. Tasha had hardly gone out since breaking up with Jeff. It was Claire's idea to get Tasha to go to Bob's gallery opening. Tasha was so nervous, Claire remembers how it took her three hours to choose what to wear, three hours to decide on too much foundation, too much eye shadow, a black cameo choker, an old Victorian lace blouse, a long skirt and leggings, and over all this an old belt of Jeff's, which to Claire's mind made Tasha look even skinnier. Claire closes her eyes as she recalls her suggestion that they smoke a joint with Bob before they went. Another mistake, for whenever Tasha got high she got unstable. She flirted with everyone, trying to have all the attention, bumming cigarettes from Liz, drinking constantly, smiling madly, swinging her head back and forth like a giraffe when other people spoke. God, she looked out of it. A few days before she told Claire that people know she's crazy. "Guys take me out twice and never call me again," she said. "They can smell my neuroses a mile away." So that night at the gallery she was attempting to prove to everyone that she could enjoy a normal night out. Standing with her near the bar, Claire had a brief, nurturing compulsion to guide Tasha to the buffet. Claire told her that she had a fantasy about a long room with tables, and on the tables were all the meals she'd ever eaten. She told Tasha she imagined she could simply go in and take whatever she wanted. Tasha had stood there, quiet, a faraway look in her eyes and a twisting, satisfied smile on her lips, as if she were somewhere else. Claire, instantly furious, remembered Patrick talking about Tasha: "Ratty-rat's problems are all self-indulgent, bourgeois affectations." In the gallery, for that one second, Claire agreed with him. But then Tasha grabbed Claire's arm and told her she had to go home. She had a migraine, she said, and couldn't look at people anymore. She could see right through them, she said, she could see the crackers and mushrooms and red peppers being chewed in their mouths and in their stomachs and in their digestive tracts. She had to leave the party, she said, and the two of them went home, where Tasha threw up for the rest of the night.

Liz comes back from the kitchen. "Okay," she says, "I'm going to call my parents then I'm going to call the landlord and tell him if he hasn't already cashed the rent cheque, not to cash it till Tuesday. Then I'll make a deposit with Bell so we can have a phone. And then I'm calling Tasha's parents."

Claire, on the sofa, looks up. "You can't call her parents, Liz."

Liz says nothing.

"Her family's too fucked-up."

"Everybody's family's fucked-up."

"Yeah, but Tasha's mother has so many guilt trips flying around, Tasha throws up every time she talks to her. You know that."

"Well, she can't make me throw up. Look, Claire, I'm not supporting Tasha's anorexia anymore. And I'm certainly not subsidizing it. Her parents can do that if they want. I'm calling them right now and I'm going to ask them for the eight hundred dollars Tasha owes us."

Claire jumps off the sofa and runs to the kitchen. She takes the phone bill that Liz has just taped to the fridge and returns to the living room. "Here," she says, pointing to a long-distance number. "That's Tasha's sister in Hamilton. You should call her instead."

Liz looks at Claire and takes the bill. "You know," she says, moving toward the door, "this isn't our fault, Claire. It's not our fault that she's addicted to sorrow and misery and pain ... It just isn't."

"Yeah," says Claire. "But there is something called compassion when people aren't perfect." Liz is already halfway down the stairs; Claire doubts she heard her.

Claire lingers in the doorway, wondering how much of the conversation Tasha has overheard. She pictures Tasha in the bathroom, sitting on the floor with her hands over her ears, hating Liz, glad that Liz is moving out ... And what if Liz does go? Claire begins to imagine how their lives will shift away from each other, Liz getting a bachelor apartment, finishing her Ph.D. in a carrel at the library, frowning as students like Claire slide late essays under her door ... And Tasha, her parents arriving to get all her stuff, finding the giant box hidden in Tasha's closet, the box full of back issues of *Vogue*, old perfume bottles, piles of unread political theory books and feminist novels, and all Tasha's shoes, shoes she buys but never wears, unpacked, untouched, pristine in their boxes ... Tasha retreating further into herself, maybe losing more weight and having to be hospitalized and fed intravenously, like when she was sixteen. Tasha, whom Claire has always thought the brightest, the most beautiful, the most talented ... But now Claire doesn't know where Tasha will be in a few years. Claire has always believed that they were going to be all right, that they would all look back on these years and fondly remember the chaos and poverty. Now she isn't as sure, and the chaos and poverty are beginning to frighten her with their persistence. Suddenly staying up all night with Bob seems grossly impractical. Claire stands up straight and takes a breath. She knows she is moving into that mood where she worries and worries and worries and soon she'll be worrying about all her friends and her family and her Catholic moody mother and her sister and her lovers ...

She walks down the hallway and into her bedroom. There are clothes everywhere, on the floor, on the bed, hanging off the chair, stuffed in a plastic recycling bin in the corner. With a rush of energy, she gathers them up and drops them in the centre of the bed. She opens her closet and pulls from a rubber boot a mason jar full of pennies and a few quarters. She places this together with the clothes and ties the four corners of the bed-sheets in a knot. She slings this sack over her shoulder and starts down the hallway. Then, surprised that the bathroom door is open, she drops the sack and is about to unbutton her jeans when she stops and returns to her room. She grabs a pill-bottle from underneath her bed and rinses it in the bathroom sink. Then she sits on the toilet and starts to pee. Unable to stop, she fills the pill bottle, the warm overflow rushing across her fingers.

Will Waiting

IT'S ONLY A TEST, RIGHT? I can go tomorrow. It's not crucial I go today. But today is the day it's ready, right, and if I put it off, it's like I'm scared, like I'm avoiding it, and things that you're scared of have power over you, and I'm the fucking one who should be in control, right? Have to run my own life. I'll go downstairs, have some breakfast, and then I'll drop by. No. What I should do is join the Y and then go. Weights, the pool, squash, worry. Like Bigley, always worrying. I don't know how to play squash. I'll learn. The new and improved Will Weston. I look good in shorts.

Eight forty-five. Half an hour. If I get up now I can have breakfast and do the Y-tour before ten. They said come at ten. The tenth hour. God what a fucking life. Spend your childhood learning about secrets and shame, settling for counterfeit affection, being funny or smart or talented before coming out on the side of honesty, and just being, out in the open, living freely and doing your thing when one day you feel tired, go to some clinic and listen to a doctor with rubber gloves talk about risks and protection and exposure, treatments and years and mortality statistics and suddenly everything's different and nothing's the same. And then I think what the fuck am I doing? This is my life. I've worked hard to have my life and I intend to make it better. I can't afford any of this.

What if it's positive? Support systems, families and friends, drug plans, and—oh fuck I can't believe I'm doing this. Let's add up all the people who love me and see if it's enough. Mom, Dean, Kay, Rodney—what about Gary, friend of

Rodney's? He tested positive six years ago and he's doing fine. He's fine. But that skinny lawyer guy, he came to see the show closing night, sat in the front row and told us how beautiful the set was, squinting at the actors, his hand too fucked-up to hold the programme, Rodney had to keep picking it up for him. I don't want to think about all this. A lot of people have been walking around for twelve years and they're perfectly healthy.

But if I didn't want to think about it why'd I get tested? Maybe they only give you an appointment if you're positive. Maybe they'd've called if I was negative. Just a casual message left on my machine, like "Hello, Will. Dr. Aaktar's office calling. Have a fabulous life. Good luck with your career." Nah, she'd never do that. Too thorough.

I don't *have* to go. I could just forget about it, never pick it up. I bet some people do that. No, I'll go downstairs, pick up a paper, have a bowl of café au lait, jump in a cab to Dr. Aaktar's, and shiver in her air-conditioned waiting room like a serf. If I'm positive, she'll have reviewed my file already. It'll be on her desk. "I think you should sit down." That's how I'll know. But if she closes the door and then gets out my file, I'm fine. But Dean was negative and he still had an appointment. Why'd he get tested? It's like one day I'm not even thinking about this and then the next day I feel a little sluggish, so I pick up the phone and make an appointment. So stupid. A sudden rash of nerves—a rash. I don't want a rash, I hate rashes. I had a rash in grade six and Celie Leman made fun of me for a week. Little witch. Yeah, well, she got hers. Now she's married and lives in a trailer in Blind River with three kids and an alcoholic. Divine retribution. God, everyone from high school will think I died like a faggot in the city. Except Shelley Chiasson. She was nice. She was the only cool person who was nice. Like when that guy from Worthington Street died, I didn't even know he was a fag. God, maybe he wasn't, maybe he was a junkie. I'm just as bad as the rest of them, making assumptions. I mean if I think like this, what does Pat Buchanan think? Maybe that guy was just unlucky or careless, everybody's careless sometimes. The cost of an erection. What was that guy's name? He was in my French class. *Gaston Gavroche, enfant terrible. Il mange tout le gâteau. Pitou, Pitou, es tu un chien méchant? Et tu, Pitou? Et Brute?*

Rodney said why get tested unless you're sick. Rodney's right, of course. Rodney's always right. "Will, why are you obsessing about this?" Why, indeed. It's a way of life—aah—I mean it used to be. But you know if I was American, I'd have to pay three thousand bucks for the test. It'd be awful. Who looks after those people? Maybe there'll be a cure. Maybe I should cancel. Maybe I shouldn't have done this. I don't know, though. I should have. I could have. If only I'd. Why didn't I. Fuck, my heart feels like I just ran a marathon.

Nine o'clock. T minus one hours. I'm lying here thinking about getting it, aren't I? Button button who's got the button? Now I'm one of those people who stares at their ceiling and worries. How many times have I looked at this cracked stucco ceiling? How many moods? Goddamn virus, disease, condition, whatever the fuck it is. Ah, I'm sick of it. If I'm sick, I'm sick, if I'm not, I'm not. I'm either going to get sick or I'm not. God, Mom. I can't put Mom through that. She'd be crushed. Just what she wants to hear. The phone call she's been waiting for. No, I don't care. I'm not getting it and that's that. I refuse. I've been careful. Almost always. I have to be hopeful. Optimistic. Realistic. Right. What if it's negative, what then? Do I celebrate or buy a pair of runners? But even if I do test negative, I wouldn't believe it. Not really. Humans are scared. But really, after all this is over, I'll use this angst to turn my life around. And later I won't forget what a glib asshole I've been to people, they sure won't. A new beginning. Love and compassion. Love and compassion. That's my future. And humour. Love and compassion and humour. I'll spread it through the world. Frosting for the world cake. No matter what. Too much goddamn suffering. I hate suffering, I wasn't meant for it. Even as a kid I ignored it. Frost bite, cuts and bruises, nothing more than insults. My father taking me skiing, *tha*t was suffering, my big father who still can't say the word gay. I guess that's suffering, too. Everyone in denial. World denial. Honesty is the answer to life. But I'll do it. I'll join the Y. I'll drink fruit juice. I'll drink beet juice. I'll drink million-dollar organic vegetable juice from Noah's Health Foods. I'll have one as soon as I get up, before I see the doctor, before I go to the Y, just to show my commitment. I'm going to be healthy no matter what. Exercise, rotations, push, strain, sweat. Ugh. What's a couple of antibodies when you're young?

Okay, how many times was I unprotected? Let's see. I don't think I want to do this. Stephano and all the—I didn't even know who he was. What was I thinking? How nice it would be to feel his beautiful strong hands on my ass, is what I was thinking. How his rich wet mouth, no, no, stop, not now. I'm never having sex again. I'm only wanking. Stephano, oh God, poor Stephano, just got a little out of hand, had a couple of problems. Love and compassion. Why am I worrying about him? He's going to be a total star art boy. If he were sick, his stuff would sell better. But he's fine. I'm fine, right? I can't believe this. I wasn't even worried when I went. It was an impulsive thing and now here I am lying in bed afraid to get up, afraid I have unwittingly changed my life. *Oh please*. God, this is serious, though. I have to remember this for serious-guy roles ... Oh, no. There'll be a musical. As soon as one of Andrew Lloyd Webber's friends die, there'll be a musical.

I don't know, I don't know, no one really knows anything. All those meetings I spent being bored or chatting someone up ... okay, two meetings. So I'm a narcissist not an activist, surprise, surprise. But all the people talking, like actors, me thinking of it as an act somehow, a photograph or something not quite real. Bigley standing in movie line-ups, pointing at people. "He looks good, doesn't he? He's been so sick. He looks great for seven years. He used to be so thin. It's the macrobiotic supplements and Vitamin C. Oh and look, I hear he's been really sick but he has this guru from Boston who ..." All the buzzwords. "Septra ... yeast ... visualization therapy ... he had the worst case of ... his theory is that ... viral soup ... infections ... steroids ... chronic management ... Wellesley Hospital ... palliative care ... see the sunburn ... it was really extraordinary ... his doctor says that ... hepatitis, herpes, warts ... diagnosed in February ... cell growth ... direct contact ... latency period ... you should think about it like this ... they said meningitis but you know what that means ... lupus ... patents ... vaccines ... sarcomas ... opportunistic infections ..."

What does that mean, opportunistic? It can't think, it has no strategy, it's just a—what is it? Does it even exist? One globule of fluid teeming with microbes, tiny little thing, but it's enough, it'll do. Fuck, you can't help thinking of it as if it were intelligent, some alien life form, some sentient being. It's just a thing, or is it a state? What does it look like? T-cells. Tea sells. He sells T-cells by the sea shore. By the street whores. To those who need more. Oh boy. T-cell: (tee sel), *noun*, a small M&M-like microscopic structure with a capital T in its centre, found in human blood, except for the blood of people infected with what may or may not be a virus, may or may not be a condition, may or may not be a disease ...

So right now there's some guy in a lab coat, some guy looking in a microscope counting T-cells, writing down on the paper positive or negative, positive or negative. Probably a computer, though. But what if it's wrong? Plus or minus one per cent. I don't want to have to do this again.

Okay. I have to visualize the white blood cells. All the T-cells, little T-cells, fighting. Go T-cells go! Smash those fucking viruses. The whole disease thing. Too horrible to contemplate. No, it isn't. That's a stupid romantic reaction. It's either there or it isn't. Think of the thousands walking around Toronto right now who have it, never mind the thousands like me lying on their beds, staring at the ceiling, wondering. Lying in bed thinking they might die. What a cliché. I hate clichés, and now I'm stuck in one. I am one. *Cliché, c'est moi.* The latest clichés in uplifting pamphlets.

It's the city, the city's bad. It's not very healthy. What am I doing here? My parents are healthy. North Bay is healthy. I should go back to North Bay. Serve on the PTA with Shelley Chiasson, I'll be the French teacher. All that clean air, and trees and fat guys with beer and fried food. Right. The city's fine. I'm healthy. Let's be reasonable.

Alcohol? Yes. Junk food? No. Drugs? Not really. Exercise? Bicycle. Meat? Hardly ever. Cigarettes? Never. Sex? Gladly. Condoms? Mostly. Lies? Sometimes. Well, that's not so bad. But fuck, a hundred years ago you could drink, you could smoke, you could have sex and now you can't do any of those things without feeling guilty. I'm so glad I'm not twenty. Who the hell wants to be a fitness freak when they're twenty? Who wants to spend their life worrying? No wonder everyone's earnest. When I was twenty I got a little bit of life, things were swinging. The halcyon days. Now, Lord, kids grow up in the Chicken Little show. The sky is falling, the sky is, whap. One look at that and bingo, they all program their VCRs, throw on their best J. Crew and cycle to the gym to do a hundred laps, or five Ks, or a curl or two. It's true. "Wanna go for a drink?" "No, but I'll have a V8." Work and you will be saved. Reverend Alec John from St. James in North Bay. Work it together. You are a triangle, mind, body, spirit. God, maybe the Reverend John was right. The Reverend John, oh please, work and you will be saved ... Try work while you still have the light, try work out. The Reverend you-are-wrong, The Reverend I'll-Catch-Up Later, The Reverend Wait-And-See. *There are more dead people than live people*, well that's very nice, Reverend. Any more comforting thoughts about this bit-part fucking life that continues forever without you? Any advice for one dinky voice among all the souls who have ever lived? It's idiotic. We're all self-important extras. And I thought it was just Bigley. I am Bigley. *Bigley, c'est moi*. Oh God, how depressing. Bigley and everyone else will be living in the future and I'll be dead back in the twentieth century. The party's over boys and girls, life is serious now. Staying alive. Staying alive's the prize ... This is dumb. Oh my, all this worrying, I'm not made for it. This is like Kay. This is Kay's brain. Kay, she'd be devastated, what would she say? Something really smart like—Oh fuck it's nine-thirty.

Kay Returns

"WHEN ARE YOU GOING to change that message?" Kay said into the pay phone. Her hair was damp from a shower, her face pale, and there was a small reddening spot on the left side of her cheek, just beyond the rim of her sunglasses. "Hi, Will, are you there? I'm across the street. I took the red-eye this morning and guess what—I got fired! I got fired from my own movie! Isn't that great? I think I'm starting to see a pattern here. But I'm happy to be back. It was so hyper and horrible at the end. It's a totally different movie now. I mean I knew that as soon as I sold it but—and it'll probably get rewritten three more times! And last night, you should listen to this so you'll know how to be a sleaze-bag when you grow up, last night when I left, the rumour was that Junior wasn't even going to do the movie! Apparently he signs contracts to do an impossible number of movies all at the same time and then uses his out-clause to just do the one he likes best and tells the other ones to fuck off. Incredible, isn't it?" Kay brought up a hand to stifle a yawn. "It still might happen, though." The line clicked and went dead. Kay put in another quarter and called back. "You've got to change that message," she said, wiping something out of her eye. "People will think Stephano still lives there. Okay, so it's about ten-thirty now and I'm going to go to Claire's place—have you seen her? It's like she's vanished from the planet. And where are you anyway? God, I feel like I'm marooned here. So call and leave a message on my machine, okay, and—and I want to see you, for God's sake! Let's go out for breakfast or something. It's beautiful out and I'm determined to celebrate. I've been lugging this bottle of champagne around since the duty-free … So, yeah, okay, I guess that's everything. Oh—I gave your audition tape to Miles, and he said he'd look at it. So there you go. Okay. Bye."

Kay hung up and grabbed the bottle of champagne off the top of the pay phone. She walked along Bloor Street, stopping briefly in front of a window display of summer clothes. The store hadn't always been a clothing shop, Kay remembered. When Will got his apartment here five years ago, it had been a frozen-yogurt store. Before that, something else. A Hungarian restaurant, Kay thought, but she wasn't sure. She walked along, looking in the windows of the shops and cafes.

When she first moved to Toronto, she had looked at things with such urgency. Storefronts, architecture, newspaper articles, local television, all of these seemed to offer some insight into the meaning of the place. She remembered when she first encountered the words "North Toronto" and her confusion upon hearing them, knowing by the tone of voice that North Toronto was more than a geographical description. All the things she had thought necessary to learn, the different high schools, the universities, the magazines, the bars, the restaurants, the neighbourhoods …

Over the years, she had learned the city's vocabulary, she had learned about its money, its ambitions, its limits. But walking past these shops Kay realized that this vocabulary did not make her any more at home; the city had simply ceased to be foreign. She moved the champagne to her other arm and continued walking. There was a dog barking somewhere.

Kay turned down Palmerston and was relieved to see Claire's bicycle locked to the railing on the front porch. She went around to the back of the house and, looking up the stairway, saw that the door to Claire's apartment was open.

"Claire?" Kay called out, taking off her sunglasses. "Hello?" But, except for a scuffle in the bathroom, which revealed itself to be the cat, there was no answer. In fact the apartment seemed empty, neglected somehow. Kay, wondering if one of the room-mates had just stepped out for a second, noticed that the wall, where the blue painting had hung, was bare.

"Claire?" Kay called again. She flicked on two light switches but both lights were burnt out. She went to the kitchen and tried the phone; still dead.

"Hello?" she tried again, quite loudly. The cat, who had followed her into the kitchen, sniffed at Kay's shoe, then disappeared under the table. Kay plunked her bottle on the counter and opened a cupboard. A bag of chocolate chips sat beside a lopsided, home-made coffee mug. She grabbed the mug and closed the cupboard, then opened it again and snatched some chocolate chips. Pushing the melting chocolate around with her tongue, she twisted the cork off the bottle and poured the champagne. She looked sternly at the home-made mug as if she didn't trust it, then drank off the champagne in one toss. She poured herself another.

There was a faint organic smell coming from somewhere in the apartment, as if someone had left a half-eaten apple on a windowsill or in a waste basket. Kay gazed briefly at the grubby kitchen counters before she yawned a face-distorting, five-second yawn, grabbed her mug of champagne and walked in a vague, graceless—almost purposefully awkward—way down the hall to Claire's bedroom. Behind her, the cat nosed the front door open and scooted down the stairs.

Claire's room, surprisingly, was spartan. The window was wide open, the bed stripped, and except for a single sports sock on the floor, there were no clothes anywhere. Bending down on one knee, Kay searched around the bed. She picked up a guitar pick, then, dissatisfied, moved over to the desk. A winter's worth of dust had collected on its surface, accenting the solid dark circles left by cups and glasses. The computer screen was dark, there were no pens or pencils, just two five-and-a-quarter-inch computer disks and a pad of yellow paper. Standing over

the desk, Kay picked up the pad of paper and began reading
what was written in black ball-point pen on the top page:

Through Male Eyes:
Ethical Theory and Women's Moral Development

Ethical theorists and psychological theorists of
moral development have traditionally separated
the spheres of ethics and politics, in the sense that
they haven't taken account of the power relations
between moral agents. That is, they have generally
assumed that the ethical actions, the subjects of the
theory, are in a position of equality. However, to
separate the spheres of ethics and politics is, as
Rousseau said, to make both disciplines incompre-
hensible. The Feminist slogan, "the personal is
political," is a recognition of the fact that "private"
ethical decisions and actions inevitably have public
repercussions.

Traditionally, theories of moral development
have been formed by men, and through studying
men, yet have been applied unisexually. Moreover,
given the fact that language is patriarchally con-
structed, what kinds of procedures can best be followed to properly re-evaluate existing socio—
what recourse have women that sexual recognition
of differentiation This paper seeks to
—(subvert the social structure)
—undermine the moral implications of the action
—moral implications
—Hermeneutics
—post office
—phone bill

laundry
tea bags
Bookshelf from PP
deodorant!
light bulbs
bagels
bank

And here, about two-thirds of the way down the page, the writing stopped. Kay took two steps backward, the pad of paper in one hand, the mug of champagne in the other and sat on the edge of Claire's bare bed. She flipped the first page over and looked at the pages underneath. These pages had been written much more quickly. The handwriting style switched from slanted to vertical to back-slant with each paragraph.

March 25

Dearest Kay,

Sorry, sorry, sorry this has taken so long. I've just been finishing what seems like a hundred essays before the end of term, not to mention that the rest of my life kind of erupted around me and had to be shovelled back into its volcano—all of which has taken the last week or so.

So here are your files. I hope I have the right one. I misplaced your letter so I just copied all the files that had the word MAYA in them, that's why there's two disks. And plus, when I went to get the disk, I finally took that white blouse back from Liz and I left it on your bed. Sorry she kept it for so long. Sometimes, Liz likes things so much it's impossible to get them back.

And I think just making the decision and going to LA was really smart. Of course it's sad you couldn't make it yourself, but you'll have money and like you said it won't be the last thing you'll ever do. I was kind of looking forward to seeing Maya in the snowstorm, though; it's a bit sad no one will ever see that scene. I mean it was very dreamy and ethereal and non-profit but it was always the thing that stayed with me most. I always filled in the rest of the film on either side of it. Besides, it might be better to know that you have a snowstorm that never existed. But you will have money and you'll be able to take taxis everywhere! And we can go to Mexico! Back to the yoga camp! What do you say?

Anyway, it's finally warm here again. The windows are unfrozen so you can open them and the wind's full of snow melt and slushy dirty puddle smell. Makes you want to sweep. So I did: dust bunnies galore in the corners breeding toenail clippings, pubic hairs and miniature cheeseburgers. Next week: the bathroom.

Best love,
Claire

P.S. Could I get Judith's number from you? Since you're not seeing her anymore, I think it would be a really good idea for Tasha to talk to someone who knows more about things than Liz and I. And plus I really want to

Kay turned the page to see if there was anything else. There wasn't. She took a sip of champagne then set the mug beside her foot and lay back on the bed. She brought up the pad to reread the letter but her eyes focussed past its pages, on the ceiling. She looked at the water stains, trembling cobwebs and flaking paint. For a short while she traced a system of cracks around the ceiling, then she turned her head and stared out the open window. In a nearby tree, a squirrel leapt easily from one branch to another before disappearing. Kay watched until the two branches stopped shaking. Then, as the sun passed behind a cloud, she lifted the pad off her chest and looked at it once more. She wanted to read the whole thing again, the essay, the list, the letter, but in another few moments she had closed her eyes and let the pad fall to her side. "Mexico," she said to no one, then she fell asleep.

Almost twenty minutes later, a door opened in the apartment. Tasha, wearing a baggy kangaroo sweatsuit, came out of her room. She padded down the hall in heavy wool socks, her sweat pants tucked inside the socks and her sleeves tucked inside her fists. Standing quietly in Claire's doorway, Tasha could see Kay asleep on the sheetless bed, Kay's slightly opened mouth the source of a slow but steady snore. For a full minute Tasha watched the other woman sleeping, then she closed the door and walked back down the hall. There was a tiny hole in the tip of her sock.

By The Way

ONE OF THE WEIRDEST days of my life, Friday April 3, 1992, actually began the day before. I'd gone to Bob's to return his painting, and we stayed up all night drinking gallons of red wine and talking about love and babies and destiny. Bob adores me. I can tell he wants me to move in with him and if ever I could sense a guy thinking he wanted to marry me, Bob was him. Which is an odd feeling to have at twenty-four. He just liked me too much, and the commitment he was willing to make was way too serious. It was exhausting even contemplating it. It was great for my ego and everything, but it was maybe a bit out of proportion to the time we spent together, and the thing was, his room-mate kept coming on to me and that was like a big problem. So I left Bob's at about seven in the morning and proceeded to fall asleep on the subway and miss my stop. I woke up at Royal York station with a raging ear infection (the doctor told me I should always wear ear-plugs when I go swimming but I find this difficult and depressing because if I don't wear my contacts it's a Helen Keller kind of situation so you can understand why I tell myself it's okay to swim without them) and just as I was waking up, I heard a voice in my dream say, "a thousand tangerines." I have no idea what it means, but the tone of voice was like "Is there any more coffee?" or "Are you Claire Pritchard?" or "Excuse me, you're on my foot," and it repeated in my head like a metronome for the rest of the day.

So I came home very blissed out and calm and walked into this big fucking confrontation about Tasha with Liz. For the last couple weeks, Tasha had been in this hibernation routine where she never went out, didn't talk to Liz, and only talked to me from behind her door. She used to freak if you went into her room when she wasn't home—like Liz and I were going to run in and smell her bras or something—and then she just stopped going out altogether and kept all this food under her bed and essentially skulked around in greasy hair like a mad-woman in the attic.

Liz had a little fit, said she had to move out and stomped off. I was standing there, furious that Liz was being so anal and authoritarian about everything, hating that she probably thought Tasha and I were sappy, weak, self-destructive women. Rather than wait for Liz to come back, I decided to do the laundry that I'd been avoiding for the last year. So after refilling my little pee-bottle, which I'd sort of made into my mascot, I went to the laundromat and realized it was going to take at least nine loads to do everything. I knew I'd have to leave my clothes unattended while I dropped off my sample at the drugstore anyway, so for a split-second I debated whether I should be one of those people who leaves their clothes in the dryer and comes back at midnight to see their stuff on top of the machines—I've always secretly admired them—but then I remembered how Jacob had all his clothes stolen in Jerusalem so instead I paid the laundry people to do it. It left me with fifty-one dollars to my name, but to tell you the truth, I didn't want to contend with a whole winter's dirty laundry, plus the idea of fighting people for dryers was just too dispiriting.

So I dropped off my pee at the drugstore and went for a coffee at By The Way, a café I usually avoid, even though everyone else is devoted to the place, especially Tasha, who used to go there religiously because she thought one of the waiters was cute. I just don't think it's worth paying three bucks to have cinnamon in your coffee whether you like it or not. But that morning it was sunny and bright and beautiful and suddenly I felt like I just wanted to sit down. So there I was, sitting in the window, kind of spacing out, watching people go by—people I kept thinking I recognized—and looking at little pods of sunlight on the table. They were kind of entrancingly beautiful, the way the light refracted into different colours. I was arranging my creamers so that their shadows had little haloes when I slipped into a daze. I get this feeling when I'm really, really tired. I can't articulate it, and I can never recall what it's like until it happens—I used to get it a lot as a kid when I was falling asleep. It's this sensation where I smell licorice candies and miniature thumbs massage the roof of my mouth. And when it happens, my mind goes green and I can keep track of about five different thoughts at once. I know it sounds very schizzy, but to me it's very soothing. I mean I often have this general, all-purpose anxiety about things—like do I have bad breath, did I just say something stupid, do I look too ugly, how bad are my roots showing, is this person going to hate me (I used to go crazy thinking there might be people out there who hate me; and I suppose there probably are), I mean usually my thoughts fly off in a hundred different directions. But when I'm overtired like this, it's a very peaceful, tranquil state of mind I have, and in By The Way I could feel myself getting little ESP glimmerings where I could see things very clearly. Like I suddenly knew why Patrick was wrong about Tyborg.

Patrick makes this noise in his nose whenever he thinks something is overrated. It sounds like "mfft." It means if-you-knew-a-little-bit-more-about-this-you-would-know-not-to-like-it, and it drives me crazy. It's good to like things when you're alive, and it's good to show people that you like them. That, to me, should not be pre-empted or precluded; what's good is the liking. I firmly believe that. I'm not saying never be critical, but mffts are not critical, mffts are just hateful. I know Patrick is not the only person who's like this, but there were just too many times when I shared in his snooty point of view like a good protective girlfriend and that bugs me. That can be the tyranny of going out with someone, that all you end up doing is preserving and protecting their point of view.

Patrick. It's so strange for me to think of our relationship now. A while ago, if someone mentioned his name, it wouldn't have meant anything to me. And now, I've *lived* with him. I went from not knowing him to screwing him and having breakfast with him and moving in with him, all in a year. It seems ridiculous now. I hate that, though, that your relationships with people seem ridiculous to you a year later. I mean, Patrick and I, we'll probably drift apart and lead different lives and not see each other anymore, till he just winces when he hears my name. But it makes me think that I won't see people anymore, that all my friendships will gradually dissolve or get replaced, and it makes me feel that coinciding with other people's lives doesn't last very long. Like with Jacob, for a while we were each other's favourite person in the world, and now we don't even write. Hardly a day used to pass without me thinking of him, like reading his horoscope or wondering what he'd think of the brother who married his sister on "Oprah," and now I can't even tell you where he is. I never thought life would be so transient and unresolved. I remember in grade eight my mother wondering why Kay never saw her best friend Jill Keating anymore, and Dad saying, "People drift apart" in a defeated kind of way, and I remember wondering how he came to that conclusion. How long do you know people?

I mean Henley's going on tour with Sleeping Dogs in June, and it doesn't take a genius to figure out that a million girls are going to fall in love with him. He did ask me to go with him, and I might still meet him in New York for New Year's, but I don't want to lose another year of my life traipsing across the country being The Girlfriend. I won't really be seeing Bob either, because it would be too hard on him and Pruey's moving to Montreal … I think maybe I liked the idea of Pruey more than I liked Pruey herself. I love that she's one of those people who doesn't surprise you if she buys a motorcycle and drives to Argentina, or becomes a Montessori teacher, or gets married and moves to Berlin. I love that after a lifetime of everyone telling her what beautiful red hair she has, she got a crew cut and dyed it black. And I love that I once saw her chase two guys down the street and kick them after they whistled at her. But I don't know if I make the best lesbian-girlfriend in the world. The night I slept with her, after Henley fell asleep, Pruey and I stayed up and she was surprisingly different from the way I thought she'd be. Wonderfully surprisingly different, but for a couple seconds I felt like she really wanted me to be in control, and that made me feel like I was watching myself on TV and I have this rule that if I'm watching myself on TV, it means I don't really want to be there. I kind of love Pruey, though, and I'm glad I slept with her. She's an inveterate spooner.

I wish Pruey'd met Tyborg. I wish I'd introduced them. In fact, stirring my coffee, I was thinking I should have introduced a lot of people to each other, and then I looked out the window and saw Kay's friend Will on the sidewalk. I see him in the strangest places. I won't see him for a year, and then we'll see each other five times in the same week. He was right outside on the sidewalk and he didn't see me, so it was like I was watching him through an observation window. He had a carton of orange juice in his hand, and I watched him lift it up and drink till it was empty.

I have never known what Will thinks of me, like if he's horrified to see me or what. And because I'm kind of intimidated by him and want to impress him, I'm either a babbling conversational prostitute around him or a really quiet hippie-dippie girl. My anxiety meter usually bumps up when I see him, but maybe because I was so drop-dead tired, it was just like, oh, there's Will.

I watched him toss the juice carton in the garbage can and squint down the street, like he was looking for a taxi or waiting for someone to pick him up. Then he turned around and came in By The Way. He immediately had to scrunch up next to me to let the waiter go by. When people are really, really close to me, like when I can smell their shampoo or see the pores on their nose, sometimes I get this overwhelming idea that I'm going to kiss them in the next second, so my left hand kind of reached over to touch Will's wrist. Then of course I hoped my stinkiness didn't bowl him over. I knew I smelled like B.O. and baby farts.

"Hey Claire," he said, sliding into the chair. "What are you doing?"

"Just kind of waiting around to find out what the rest of my life will be like."

"I was just wondering the same thing. Half an hour ago. Did you just write an exam?"

"Yeah, that's why I'm sort of in bag-lady mode." I didn't have the guts to keep lying, though. "I'm actually waiting around to get the results of a pregnancy test."

"Oh. I thought you did that."

"Yeah, I don't think it was too reliable. So I tried on all my pants and skirts to see which ones fit and which ones didn't and—"

"And?"

"They don't fit. I can't even fit into my plaid skirt. So I'm finally breaking down and using western medicine."

Will smiled. He was really easy-going and calm. I wondered if he was always like this, and I just never noticed before. I think I've always thought he was really springy and manic because the first time I met him at York he monopolized the whole night and I thought he was the funniest person I'd ever met.

"You pick up the results today?"

"Yeah," I said. "Same day service. Which is great. It's ideal for me obviously."

I saw a woman go by the window. I asked Will if he knew her. He turned to look but she was gone.

"She's this beautiful actress," I said. "I've been seeing her everywhere. I think you know her. Kay and I saw her one night and since then I literally haven't gone a day without bumping into her."

The waiter came, the cute one, and Will ordered a bowl of café au lait with chocolate. "So when are your results ready?"

"Eleven o'clock."

"The eleventh hour."

"Yeah."

"Are you going to pick it up or just call?"

"Just call."

"Do you want me to call?

"No, that's okay. Maybe. I don't know. I just want to sit and have a coffee for a second and not think about anything."

Will leaned back in his chair and pulled out some stuff from his pockets. He put some money in his shirt and a whistle in his jacket. Some day I'd like to do a photographic essay of what's in people's pockets. I'd like to make a documentary about a group of people who take the English as a Second Language exam, too. I have a lot to do on that someday.

"Have you thought about what you're going to do?" he said.

"Yeah, I kind of want to make my decision before I find out."

Will looked at his watch. "So you've got twelve minutes."

"Yeah. But in a strange way, I'm not worried about it. I just don't want to be stunned when I find out."

I really wasn't worried, that's the strange thing. I mean I know I hadn't been thinking about it as much as I should, but I've always kind of thought that if I don't want things to happen, they won't, which I know is hopelessly naïve but I still sort of think it. I really wasn't worried. I usually play all these little games with myself where I have to consider all the terrible things that could happen to me. Like whenever I get on a plane I have to consider at least once that the plane will crash, otherwise it probably will. And I have to confess that I've had this residual foreboding since I had my tarot cards read in Oaxaca, Mexico. Never have your tarot cards done, by the way, unless you're having the best day of your life and can't be depressed. I had mine done by a gloom-and-doom gypsy woman in the mountains. My main card was the devil and my second was this guy with about twenty-seven swords through his head. "You used to be lucky," she said. "Now you're sad, aren't you?" And I really wasn't, but I said, "Yeah, I am." (She could've said anything, I would've agreed.) She said I could change my luck if she lit a candle for me, but it would cost me fifty bucks, which I didn't have because I wanted to buy a blanket for my parents—they'd given me all this money to go. So of course for a year afterwards I obsessed about my luck, and every time I saw the blanket where my mom hung it up in the downstairs den, I wished I'd been selfish and lit that candle. But the blanket didn't matter to me anymore so I knew I wasn't worried.

"That's good," Will said. "You should do what you want. Why worry about things you can't change? Who wants to spend the rest of their life doing that?"

"Kay ..."

"Kay." He paused. "I'm not saying not to worry. I think it's good to worry, but you have to know what to worry about."

The waiter arrived with Will's bowl of café au lait. His first sip went down the wrong way and he started choking. When he stopped, I asked him how his play went. "Sorry I didn't see it," I said.

"That's okay. Nobody else did either."

"Hey, how's Stephano?"

"He went back to New York yesterday," he said, taking a drink. "I just spent the last hour and a half cleaning my apartment. Great artist. Bad room-mate. How's young Henley?"

So, I told him about Henley going on tour in a month, and that I probably wouldn't see him. In fact, I told him how everyone in my life seemed to be going away and that my little phase of torrid affairs was petering out. "I don't regret it, though. It's just that I'm heading into a fallow period. I don't want to have to worry for a while about liking someone or them liking me."

Will was looking out the window, holding his fingers up to the sunlight. I couldn't tell if he was listening or not. I held mine up, too, to see how they turned scarlet in the sun. Will had beautiful hands with long fingers, except on the tip of his middle finger there was a speck of blue. I asked him what it was.

"I got it playing Red Rover when I was a kid," he said. "In North Bay. It's a piece of gravel. A piece of the Canadian Shield." He looked at me. "Hey, did you ever get your tattoo?"

"Hm-mm."

"Let's see."

I pulled the neck of my shirt sideways to show the copyright symbol I got on my left breast. I kind of chickened out, really, because it's only the size of a dime. Will inspected it quite closely then he laughed and said he thought it looked terrific.

I caught a guy looking at me as he went by the window. "Do you know that guy?"

Will looked at him and shook his head.

"No, I don't either. But I thought I did ... Will, how long do you think you'll live in Toronto?"

"I don't know. Why?"

"I was just wondering. Do you see yourself as being here in five years?"

"I don't know," he said. "In five years, Claire, I'll be thirty-five."

"*A-ya.* Do you think you'll ever go to Los Angeles or someplace?"

"Yeah," he said, swirling his coffee. "I think about it. What about you?"

"I'm not going to live here forever, that's for sure. I kind of have this fantasy that I'll own a farmhouse in the Maritimes with rosemary plants and plates that don't match."

"God," Will said, "you homeless Maritimers are all alike. You all sit around in cafes sipping cappuccino, threatening to move back to Brigadoon." He smiled and looked at his hand again. "I don't know how I got this speck, actually. I always say I got it playing Red Rover, but I'm really not sure how I got it. I just remember seeing it there when I was eight." He asked me if I wanted him to be there when I phoned. I said okay and went to the back near the kitchen, to use the phone. I dialed the number and although I'm a failed Catholic and haven't gone to regular church in years, I said a little half-prayer, half-promise to God and for the first time I realized I did not want to be pregnant. Will was putting five dollars on the table when the pharmacist answered. I told her my name, staring across the room at my chair, thinking that I knew I wasn't pregnant. Then the pharmacist came back on the line and said my test was normal and—*pish*—I felt relieved but sad and suddenly so overcome with exhaustion I wanted to lay my head down with the thousand tangerines and go to sleep.

Will was standing by the door, his jacket on. He mouthed "Okay?" to me and I said, Yeah, I was okay.

"Call Kay," he said, coming over and kissing my cheek. I hung up the phone and watched him go. People were still streaming by the window. The way they were dressed, the way they glanced in, they really looked like I should know them and then I realized they were all about five years younger than me and I thought, Of course, this isn't new at all, we're just replacing somebody, just like these people are replacing us. I saw Will step off the curb and walk into the street. He and another man flagged the same taxi, and Will let the other guy take it. Instead of flagging the next one, he crossed the street and started walking the other way.

People

[*From 'Will Weston' on page 78 of* People Weekly's *special issue on* "The 25 Most Intriguing People of the Year," *Dec. 18, 1995*]

Who would have thought Cary Grant crossed with Jim Morrison could be so sexy? But Weston, who stars in CBS's runaway hit series "Lead Break," combines the best of both as Goocher Zinck, the aging rock star who tries to raise three kids while juggling a live-in catatonic drummer, PTA meetings, omnipresent groupies and a record company that won't let him retire. Blessed with twinkling ironic eyes and a shock of unruly brown curls, the thirty-three year-old newcomer shot into orbit as everyone's favorite extra-terrestrial therapist in last year's sleeper, *The Morning Man*, where he stole every one of his scenes without leaving a fingerprint.

"When you're with Will,' says supermodel Saskia, Weston's co-star on-screen and off, "he makes you feel like you're the smartest, prettiest, and funniest person alive and the only person he cares about." Indeed, as *LA Times* columinist Betty Yakuki comments, "Will Weston is a Grade-A flirt. He has the tantalizing ability to say yes, no, and of course all at the same time."

Canadian-born Weston now makes his home in LA where the show is taped. "Goocher's much more laid back than I am," he concedes. "He's used to having women throw themselves at him. Me? I couldn't even get a date in high school." Well, this six-footer's sure come a long way. When he is not working on set, he's working out at the gym or exploring the coast in his Karmann Ghia. "This is all pretty new to me," he says, adding: "You know the funniest thing about playing Gooch? Up until now, I'd never even picked up a guitar." Maybe. But he's playing all the right notes now.

Kay at Last

KAY STANDS AND PULLS open the curtains. Sunlight streams into her living room, washing into the corners, illuminating specks of dust that, invisible a moment ago, now float conspicuously in the slanting shafts of light. A box full of loose paper sits in the middle of the floor. She rummages through it, stopping now and then to read a few pages. Near the back of the the pile she finds a crushed book of stamps. She takes a stamp and tosses the rest on top of the papers. Biting off a strip of gaffer tape, she seals the box and writes OFFICE on the side with a thick blue marker. She lifts the box and sets it on top of three others stacked beside a rolled-up rug. At her desk, Kay sticks the stamp on an envelope and slips it into the pocket of her white linen blouse. She opens the morning newspaper. On the third page of the arts section, in the lower right-hand corner, is an advertisement for a new movie. She bends her head down, looking for show times and studying the small print of the credits below the title. Still looking at the newspaper, she reaches for her pen and notepad. Uncapping the pen, she jots down a few words, then gets up, grabs her keys and is out the door.

All the quick ideas in her head, glittering like fish in sunlit water. An idea for this, a story for that ... These ideas, they come and go, and Kay worries if she doesn't write them down she will lose them. She used to carry them in her head, moving from one to the other, trying to keep each in motion, like a performer spinning plates on thin poles, hoping that when she returned each would still be there. For when she realizes she has forgotten something, she feels a sudden despair, as if it reminded her of her own inadequacy or demise. It is not the loss that irks her (the idea often returns), but the unwelcome possibility that no matter how hard she tries, it may not be enough.

Walking up Church Street, Kay tilts her face to catch the midday sun. There is something different about the sun here, the way it winks in and out of the clouds, it seems higher in the sky—a different quality of light, too, different from LA, less violet, and certainly different from the unbroken skies in New Brunswick. Kay takes the letter from her pocket and drops it in the mailbox at the corner of Church and Carlton. She raps the top of the box twice, then squats down to look at the headlines in a vending machine. Her boot feels loose, though she sees it's still tied. "Boots," her grandmother had said. Kay hears her voice again, as she has been hearing it these last weeks. "I waited all my life to get out of boots like that." Grandy in the hallway, watching Kay tug at a boot in the back porch, the hockey play-offs on in the next room ... Kay stands in the street, waiting for a break in the traffic. "There's nothing for us to go back to now," she'd told Claire as soon as she heard. And though it wasn't true, it frightened her to think it could be. When she came here for university, Kay could not have foreseen how far it would take her from New Brunswick. A car stops for her to cross. She squints at the brilliant reflection of the sun in its windshield, seeing in her mind stretches of marsh and woods and shoreline, the deserted clapboard houses along the Atlantic coast, all the abandoned Maritime houses, the weathered old shingles, the sagging roofs, rain falling through grey empty windows ... The laces on her left boot flap against the pavement. Kay ties them in a bow, stands up and passes through the glass doors of the movie theatre.